Christopher Hope was
Well-known as a poet
(South Africa) and the
His first novel, *A Separ*
Granada Paperbacks)
Memorial Prize. Two c
published by London
(1974) and *In the Country of the Black Pig* (1981). *Private Parts* was awarded the Silver Pen Award for the best book of 1982 by P.E.N.

By the same author

Fiction

A Separate Development

Poetry

Cape Drives
In the Country of the Black Pig

CHRISTOPHER HOPE

Private Parts

and other tales

PANTHER
Granada Publishing

Panther Books
Granada Publishing Ltd
8 Grafton Street, London W1X 3LA

Published by Panther Books 1984

First published in Great Britain by
Routledge & Kegan Paul Ltd 1982

ISBN 0-586-05899-0

Printed and bound in Great Britain by
Collins, Glasgow

Set in Times

For Phil Joffe

A foutra for the world and worldlings base!
I speak of Africa and golden joys.

Henry IV, Pt 2

Contents

Whites Only

In a corner of a sunny land . . . Come to our land.

'It's hot. God, but it's hot.'

The horse pulled the plough, the plough pulled the man. Flies bounced off the horse's shining brown back.

Sky like silver paper. Flick goes the tail.

'Jissus, but it's hot.'

Veld grass smeared across the land like mustard, windmill away to the right, a silver spoon.

This land is our land!

The man stopped the horse and loosed it from the plough. Flick, flick. A light wind. No sound. He walked to the truck parked on the edge of the ploughed field. The seat squeaked.

The red dust parachuted out behind the truck.

An unkempt little *piccanin* ran to unhook the big farm gate. The truck chugged and waited.

The *piccanin* wrestled with the wire loop on the gate post. It pinched his fingers and he grunted.

The man revved the engine.

'Stupid,' he thought.

The gate swung open and he burst through it.

'O great white light of the West,' thought the *piccanin*, gazing at him.

He drove into the six o'clock sun. The truck was a beetle, a swift *tok-tokkie* carrying him nimbly. Soon he could see the farmhouse. His belly rumbled a welcome.

'Stupid,' he told himself. But none the less he was pleased to be almost home.

He stopped at the farm gate. The sign on the fence read *Forward*! The farm had once been called *Rest and Peace* but Grannie had it changed soon after his second brother had gone to his room. That was many years ago.

He hooted several times. The broken notes, visible in the heat, floated across the yard disturbing the dirty ducks that played by the pond formed over several years near the kitchen door by seepage and infrequent rains.

A black man wearing an elegant grey suit and highly polished brown and white golf shoes appeared and carefully crossed the yard toward the gate, halting every few steps as an excited duck flung itself across his path. It was Solomon, the boss boy. His progress was that of a man crossing a busy street. He opened the gate and bowed low as the truck passed through.

'Go well, little god'; he saluted.

The man parked the truck under the eaves as he usually did and strode into the house. The kitchen was large and cool. Several cook girls prepared food at the blackened range. There was a good smell. His belly rumbled again. The women giggled. He scowled and stamped into the dining room. A woman sat on a sofa. He took off his hat and rubbed his nose.

'Hullo Grannie.'

She was tall. Her white boots touched the tops of her thighs and zipped up the back. Her hair was greying but very fine. She smiled up at him and her tongue was the colour of her blouse.

'My poor boy must be hungry.'

'Yes, hungry.'

'Your food is almost ready.'

He nodded vigorously. The gurgle in his belly was a racket in the still room.

'We must talk together,' he said hesitantly.

'Not now,' she said briskly but pleasantly. 'First eat. I will see the girls in the kitchen. Your brothers will be hungry too.'

His heart warmed to her. She was the most pleasant person he knew.

'*Ja.*'

He went to wash. When he came back into the room a place had been laid at the table and his food, covered by a plate, was waiting on his red doily. He ate rapidly and without thinking. Afterwards he sat on the sofa and smoked his pipe. He could hear Grannie collecting his brothers' plates.

He had two older brothers. Their rooms were in the long passage leading to the sun-parlour. A part of the house not used much. Neither brother had come out of his room for many years. Both were busily writing, Grannie said. She fed them three times a day, pushing a tray through the hinged hatch which each brother had made in his bedroom door. The food was received without comment.

He realized something important must have driven his brothers to their rooms. But he had been very young when it happened. Grannie knew and had laughed softly when he once asked her about it, but told him nothing.

Each brother received mail but never sent any. Two bulky parcels arrived each month with the address printed in green ink, postmarked Pretoria. Some years ago when he had been bolder he had secretly pried open one of these parcels with cold fingers. Inside was a pile of crisp, new, picture stories from the *Romantic Library*. He had never looked again.

Nowadays he no longer even remembered the names of his brothers. Indeed, he occasionally forgot about them for as much as a week at a time. But inevitably the sound of a flushing toilet late at night would issue through the quiet farmhouse to remind him.

No one else knew about his secret brothers. The farm was isolated. It perched on the border of a Bantustan. He could see the fences from his bedroom window.

Outside the drums began to knock. It was a common sound. They were turned out by a small factory some miles away and sold in great quantities to the people in the Bantustan.

He could hear Grannie moving about in another part of the house. Her boots thumping the boards gave out a sound not unlike that of the drums. The room was darkening. In the farmyard someone shouted.

'We must talk,' he called out, 'and perhaps even play some games later.'

Grannie answered unintelligibly.

He had a compendium of games. Often they would play together after dinner. Grannie's face went red when she won and she would drink to her winnings. Her favourite game was Ludo. She frowned on cards.

He put his feet upon the *riempie* table and dozed. He dreamt he saw a signpost on which were painted the names of all the bishops in Southern Africa.

He awoke to find Grannie standing over him. She looked different, somehow newer. He peered up at her. She smiled brightly, her white teeth contrasting sharply with her pinkened lips. He realized she had made herself up. Her hair was caught behind her head with a tortoiseshell clip.

'Where are you going?'

'To the school,' she still smiled. 'Tonight we have Bantu history.'

He received this information silently although it made him angry. Grannie ran a nightschool for his farm labourers. She had done so ever since the mission school had closed down. Grannie had never liked the mission school. It had been run by nuns.

'Those . . . things! Running around in their white clothes, like tick birds. And they teach the Bantu such terrible things, and pervert their natures. Worse, the Bantu become cheeky.'

The school had closed. He sometimes wondered how Grannie had managed this. He knew she had a cousin important in Pretoria.

'I will be alone here,' he complained.

But she was firm.

'I must go. My pupils will be waiting. We have history tonight. It is very important.'

She leaned over and kissed him swiftly on the forehead. As she stooped her blouse opened and he saw her breasts, white and powdered. They seemed to him like rugby balls.

Mistaking his silence she smiled down at him and smoothed his hair.

'If you like, wait up for me. We will have a game later.'

Like rugby balls! He nodded.

When Grannie had gone, he felt self-conscious so he switched on the radio and began to fill his pipe. The set hummed briefly, whispered and came alive. The sounds it thrust into the room were strange. Something about their rhythm and cadence made him listen intently. After a few moments he identified the sounds as heavy panting interspersed with groans. It occurred to him abruptly that they came from two people in an advanced stage of sexual excitation, perhaps even intercourse.

The realization rose in him like nausea. The radio on the mantelpiece encased in its brown bakelite jacket buzzed and buzzed. He retreated to the sofa and sat stolidly. Grannie must have left it on the English programme. His lower lip trembled. His thighs felt heavy. The radio squealed and grunted. With a shout he launched himself off the sofa, but he was too late. A sudden strand of music signalled the commercial.

He swung the dial gnawing his lower lip fiercely, stopped at the sound of singing and listened. A church service. He turned up the volume.

'Stupid,' he told himself with relief.

The preacher's voice broke out of the hymn, rose like a car engine after a gear change and settled into a high steady drone, filling the room.

He settled himself. The preacher led his congregation in prayer for the national rugby team. He assumed a reverential attitude. A fly flickered about him making black holes in the air. The room enclosed him.

The sudden explosive knocking alarmed him. He listened, sitting stiffly. The sound of it mixed with the rattling drums outside and became louder and louder until it seemed the house was under fire.

The creature at the back door was tiny. About three foot tall, smiling pleasantly. He wore a pair of natty *veldskoen*, sombre blue suit, silver tie. His trousers were baggy and immensely wide at the ankle. A *bokbaard* tapering to an exquisite point adorned his chin. He wore his hair short, shaved well above the ears. Amiably he insisted upon coming inside.

The man stared. He was unaccustomed to strangers at the farm. Particularly Whites. Behind the dwarf's smiling face he saw another; long, black, pointed. A dog as tall as its master. For all the dwarf's amiability there was an authoritative cast to his chin. His eyes were brown, like the dog's.

Finally the man nodded.

Dwarf and dog moved inside and wondering he led

them into the living room. The church service was still in progress. The dwarf, perfectly at ease, sat on the sofa, his feet five inches off the floor. The dog settled beside him. The man leaned against the mantelpiece.

'I was just passing,' the dwarf explained looking about the room.

The man grunted.

'You must get lonely here. Especially with all those Blacks about.' He nodded emphatically in the direction of the Bantustan.

'I have my gun.'

The dwarf was scrupulously examining the room now, even turning around to see what was behind him as if taking an inventory or as though he had been there before and wanted to be sure that everything was as he had left it.

'Good,' said the dwarf cheerfully.

The man was becoming angry.

'Yes, good.'

The dog growled and the dwarf reached down and patted it.

'It's just as well to be on one's guard,' he remonstrated briskly.

The man said nothing.

'What religion are you?'

'Dutch Reformed.'

'I'm glad.'

The dwarf had completed his inventory. There was silence. On the radio the sermon continued.

'If He had not meant it to be, it would not be, but He did and it is . . .'

The drums had not stopped.

Abruptly, the dwarf rose.

'I must be off now.'

They walked outside. The ducks shouted darkly at their

approach. He longed to ask the dwarf who the hell he was, but could not. In the yard the dwarf stopped suddenly and grabbed the man's arm.

'Your house is very neat. It shows a woman's touch. Do you have one?'

'There is only Grannie,' he replied defensively.

'Ah,' the dwarf laughed. 'I'm too inquisitive. It will not do to become too familiar.' His grasp on the other's arm insisted on this point. They stood thus joined together in the dark for some time. Then the dwarf released him.

For a moment the man imagined he might even mount his dog and canter off. But the dwarf owned an Opel.

At first he tried to propel the animal through the back door into the car. The dog resisted. The dwarf tried twice. Then suddenly, grown infuriated, he lifted the dog in his arms and flung it bodily into the back of the car, slammed the door, rushed to the driver's seat, jumped in, paused, jumped out, waved, jumped in again and drove away.

At that moment it occurred to the man that his visitor might have been Grannie's cousin from Pretoria.

Behind him the radio directed prayers for the nation's golfers.

The yard was darker, the ducks white whispers at his feet, Flick. Grannie. He must see Grannie. She was busy. He knew how absorbed she would be and would not brook an interruption. But still she would surely want to know of her cousin's visit. After all, her cousin had not been too busy to visit her. But her teaching had become for her an overriding preoccupation and he was not sure this was for the best.

She would often say:

'It is our duty to explain to the Bantu their place and

part in the history of our country so that one day they will be able to assume a proper role in the management of their own affairs.'

And again:

'They are not bad like children. One must be firm but also cherish them. We must lead them by the hand, our grasp must be friendly but also firm. They must not be allowed to become cheeky.'

He himself had never learnt history. But when he was younger, after his eldest brother had gone to his room, on special anniversaries, Grannie would send him to fetch the old black crêpe voortrekker *kappie* from the stinkwood chest in her bedroom and setting it carefully upon her head would fold her hands in her lap and talk to him of her great-grandfather who died with Retief at the hands of the mamba, Dingaan, king of the Zulus.

He had no trouble finding the *kappie* again. It was where he remembered it to be. He took it out and admired it, rubbing it against his cheek. The feel of the roughened material made him feel considerably happier and he warmed to Grannie again. He wanted to go to her. The farmhouse encouraged him with its warm silence. She would not mind an interruption, just this once. Even if it had never happened before. He decided to keep the *kappie*.

His labourers' huts were a mile away and he walked quickly. The windmill stood to his left and the barbed wire fence of the Bantustan, to the right. He sang as he walked and in his hand he held the *kappie*. This land was his father's and his father's before him, even unto the seventh generation as the Bible said, said the *dominee* on his infrequent visits in his blue Volkswagen.

Before him were the farm labourers' huts, scattered in an oval ring. Hemmed in by the huts were rows of desks raggedly arranged. A blackboard faced the desks and two coal braziers burned on either side of it. Men sat at the desks. Grannie stood at the blackboard. He rubbed and rubbed his eyes. The history class shuffled about.

Then he saw the white boots gleaming and winking. He saw Grannie naked to the waist, her blouse tossed over a corner of the blackboard, as pink as a tongue in the fiery moonlight. Grannie among the shadows. The shadows moving about her, each movement bringing a groan from the class. Grannie's hair an army. The veld pale and ill. The whip in her hand, long and delicate. The figure crouched at her feet fire shining, shadow fading, under the whip which licked out with an exasperated sound.

The knocking drums. A great heat. The skin of his face tightened and his scalp itched. He crouched, frightened, his arms over his head. The ground shook slightly beneath his feet. The rolling wagons pitching over the rocky ground disturbed the dust. The long whips felt the brown rumps of the oxen.

He wanted to disappear inside himself. To tear open his jaws and disappear head first down his own throat.

He still held the *kappie*. With great concentration he placed it on his head and tied the long strings in a bow beneath his chin, then straightened his body and stood erect, proud, separate.

The shadowy figure advanced on Grannie. She backed away, her whip hanging like a broken arm. She stood with her back pressed against the blackboard. He could see in the firelight the circles of dark hair in the pits of her outstretched arms. Her breasts were moons. His dark eyes beneath the *kappie* regarded her brightness. He saw her lips drawn back, her tongue caught between her white teeth. The figure before her rose unhurriedly, detaching itself calmly from the shadows and seemed to float over

Grannie for a few seconds and then with a sudden grabbing movement pulled her down. Grannie gave a little shriek. And he recognized Solomon, his boss boy.

Then he could not see anything but he heard a loud click as the buckle of Grannie's belt was released. The history class was quiet and attentive.

He ran, clumsily, the air so thick he felt he must chew it. Crickets jeered. It took him a considerable time to reach the farmhouse. The moon was gone and he staggered badly. Once he fell and the *kappie* almost came off so he sat and tightened the strings before getting up. Once inside the house he went to the sitting room. The radio still played. It occurred to him that there must be an all-night service. A mighty fugue rolled through the house rattling doors.

He worked feverishly for half an hour, twice hitting his fingers with the hammer and getting paint on his clothes. He had barely finished when Grannie arrived, her boots dusty.

'Silly boy,' she kept saying. But he would not speak to her. Hard and aloof, he merely indicated the painted board above the mantelpiece . . .

* You have soured my blood.

* You have killed your father and mother and all your family.

* You have snakes in your belly.

She tried to talk to him but he sulked on the sofa and would only stare at the painted board.

'If you hate me, hit me,' she asked him. 'Like a man.' And she knelt in front of him.

'Hit me,' she insisted.

But he would not. He would do nothing. Not even tell her of her cousin's visit from Pretoria.

She became angry and tried to provoke him. Her

language grew coarse and her manner unbecoming to a White woman. His only response was to burrow deeper into the sofa and pull his *kappie* tightly over his ears.

'I am not even your real Grannie.'

She was screaming at him. But he was unaffected. His eyes never left his signboard.

Then in a fury she twice urinated at his feet and he had to lift them sharply onto the sofa to avoid the spreading pool on the floor. Yet he held to his separateness.

She cried. Finally, in desperation, she told him that she was pregnant.

At this he closed his eyes. There was nothing inside him.

Now Grannie was laughing at him. It was becoming increasingly clear to him that he could not stay where he was. It seemed best that he go to his room. The door was a stout one. It shut tightly and could be securely locked. It was a nice room. The walls and ceiling were whitewashed. It was airy and always fresh and cool.

'It would be the clever thing to do,' he told himself, nodding solemnly.

Grannie was taking off her clothes but he ignored her. He had decided. That was enough. He would start in the morning with the new day.

He pulled his knees up close to his chest and prepared to wait.

Ndbele's People

Father Ndbele came from the north, and he came as a sign. His country was a desolate place, a former native reserve, remote, drought-stricken and strikingly eroded, which had been declared a self-governing new African state by the regime in Pretoria. We white people, Father Ndbele was told by Father O'Shea, his new parish priest, seemed to have found a way of disproving the old prophecy that the poor were always with us; if the poor were too much with us then we declared them independent. Into this new, poor and independent state, as was becoming customary, a go-ahead Lebanese entrepreneur flew with plans for a prodigious casino, an enormous complex created amid some ten thousand acres of virgin veld, a multi-storey concrete and glass mountain filled with gaming tables, fruit machines, cinemas, nightclubs and discothèques and surrounded by swimming pools, tennis courts, an eighteen-hole golf course and a rugby pitch. This was the course later famous among golfers who found themselves attended by troops of curious baboons, for several holes were so situated as to be indistinguishable from the enormous private game reserve well stocked with lion and elephant which lay alongside. To this great city of fun in the veld thousands of people were expected to flock for pleasures denied them at home; to play the tables, to watch banned movies and to fall into bed with pretty black hostesses.

The entrepreneur's name was Karam. A stocky, muscular, level-eyed gangster, irritable and dark-haired, who travelled everywhere by helicopter and spoke with what he clearly imagined to be an American accent, Karam flew in to negotiate the foundation of his new casino with the young chief who was now the chief minister of the new independent, drought-stricken territory, Gabriel Shushwe, a handsome and confident young accountant who had the immediate advantage over Karam of possessing a genuine American accent picked up in the years he had followed a business administration course in Philadelphia.

He pointed out that the constitution forbade the selling of land to foreigners.

'And I should know, baby, because I wrote that damn constitution myself.'

'Maybe you lease it, then?' Karam asked.

'Sure. The constitution allows leasing of land to foreigners.'

'How about ninety-nine years?'

'I'll give you fifteen.'

'You want me to invest millions in this patch of bush in exchange for a fifteen-year lease? Come on, Chief Gabriel, give me a break.'

'Fifteen years,' repeated the chief. 'Renewable. I can't say fairer than that.'

'Such kindness – it knocks me over,' rejoined the Lebanese.

'You're welcome,' came the smiling rejoinder. 'And there will be no hidden fees, or pay-offs. In return the state will want a tooth in the proceeds.'

Karam was wary now. 'You mean a share?'

Shushwe nodded. 'Fifty per cent. Off the top.'

Karam let out an incredulous yelp. 'Off the gross? You're joking!'

'And we will have employment contracts for all my people who work for you.'

'By Jesus!' The angry Karam punched his knee painfully to help him keep his mouth shut. You didn't go into a new homeland and start abusing the chief. That was one of the first things you learned as an entrepreneur. Chief Shushwe was a greedy, grasping, jumped-up little black turd. He wanted to say that, but instead he went into his usual speech: 'You're going on the map, Chief Shushwe. A palace is going up here. There'll be everything the punter desires. From simple pleasures to sumptuous luxury. I should know,' he added confidently, 'because I got other places.' Yet traces of the anger remained though he tried to make it sound complimentary: 'By God, you got a hard nose. A real operator. A real, bloody, smart operator.'

Shushwe inclined his head graciously. 'Sure,' he said.

Father Ndbele left his dusty homeland round about the time that Karam's pleasure palace rose out of the bush and the first of the great drugged animals, elephant and rhino, began arriving in their huge wooden cages to stock the game park, and the sprinkler system was being buried beneath the rugby field. He left with a sense of heightened expectation. At the little ceremony organized to mark his departure Chief Gabriel Shushwe spoke of Ndbele as the assegai tipped with tungsten aimed at the heart of white South Africa. He pointed cut that the new aim of the church to reverse their missionary role was a welcome sign of their greater understanding of the emergent black Africa, and he pointed out, too, that this reversal in church policy coincided with a very similar move among the major banks which he applauded; appointing black managers in black branches was not only sharp business practice but it had probably been instrumental in stirring the conscience of the church and he'd like to put himself on record, he told his listeners, as welcoming the willingness the powerful institutions had shown to bury their old European prejudices and turn to black Africa in a positive and co-operative spirit. Father Ndbele, Chief Shushwe said, was going out rather as Moses had done into the land of Pharaoh, he was a sign that where bankers led, churchmen might follow. The guests peered over the rims of their wine glasses at little Father Ndbele, slender, gentle, with his delicate, fluttering fingers and his large Adam's apple, full of sudden and unexpectedly quick little half-smiles that so unexpectedly brightened his dreamy features, and they thought and perhaps some of them even wished, that Father Ndbele might have been a more substantial sign.

'You're going to run into the big heat out there,' Chief Shushwe warned.

'It's my mission,' the little priest replied simply. 'I must carry the good news to the white people; they will become my people.'

'Don't bank on it,' said Shushwe.

'Give me your blessing,' Ndbele asked his chief.

'Sure.' Shushwe punched the young priest playfully on the arm. 'Go out and crucify the bastards.'

Father O'Shea, big and burly in his black cassock, a Wexford man, with a red rawboned face and prominent but very beautiful jug ears, welcomed the young black priest to his parish. The church was reassessing, in the words of the diocesan bishop, its mission to the heart of Africa, concentrating less on converting black Africans from their far-flung pagan innocence and rather more on converting secure and white congregations from their comfortable racialism, and Father Ndbele featured as one of the shock troops in that campaign. Father Ndbele's appointment to the parish was intended to be a sign of things to come. Father O'Shea had to confess to himself, looking at the delicate young man before him, that he might have wished a rather more recognizable sign.

Despite Father O'Shea's attempts to keep his congregation together they split down the middle when Ndbele joined the parish. What no one was prepared to do was to follow Father O'Shea's line that this was a perfectly unexceptional appointment. There were those like Sam Mervyn who completely supported Ndbele's appointment and said that the time for prejudice was over and that everyone had better get used to the idea that times were changing. As a banker he had seen clear signs of it in his own business, he'd witnessed an African appointed manager of a large township branch of his bank, although this had been against his advice and to the exclusion of his own nominee, yet, as he said with a rueful smile, he'd recognized, he'd had to recognize, that times were changing. Among his supporters he listed Arthur 'Porky' Reynolds, the picture restorer, with his huge, pear-shaped face and heavy smoky eyes, whose son had entered the seminary to become a Redemptorist, as well as Tim O'Hara, the retired jockey and old Valenti, the scrap metal merchant. On the other side was Boy Stockenstroom the builder and his tough bunch. Father O'Shea saw early how the two sides were lining up. One Saturday afternoon he strolled into the church while his priests were hearing confessions, from four until six o'clock, the penitents kneeling in the last few pews on either side of the central aisle, adjacent to the confessional boxes housing their favourite priests. When people like Sam Mervyn and his friends came they would pointedly cram the pew outside the black priest's door. Then Boy Stockenstroom and his lot began arriving, dusty in their working clothes, smelling of beer from the pub and flicking the icy holy water off their fingers, peering with deliberate, mocking scrutiny at Father

Ndbele's name on the cardboard card slotted into his door, only to turn their backs contemptuously on Ndbele and his waiting penitents and move off into the opposite pew, irrespective of who happened to be hearing confession there. Stockenstroom's lot were Jeff Craskil, superintendent of the local swimming pool (who was to be run out of town in later years for interfering with little girls), Rob Butler, the brick salesman, and the violently unpredictable Colonel Pienaar. Neither side was above hissing loudly and waving over potential recruits into their pews to swell their opposing votes. Hot looks pulsed across the aisles separating the warring camps. Father O'Shea wondered if Father Ndbele had noticed the battle lines being drawn.

Sam Mervyn's wife went further and faced Father Ndbele with a question, being a determined woman who had served in the Air Corps during the war. One of the few women to qualify as a gunner although the war had never moved far enough south in Africa to reach here, she had nonetheless achieved considerable fame in 1943 when on a single summer's afternoon shooting practice the anti-aircraft squad under her command had shot down thirteen consecutive dirigibles and her picture had appeared in all the papers.

'I don't know if you realize it, Father, but it's only fair to warn you that your appointment to our parish is seen in two very different lights. There are those, like me, who welcome it, but there are others who don't want you here. It's the old question I'm afraid.'

The little priest gave his gentle smile. 'I cannot make those distinctions. A priest must be one with his people. How else can he lead them out of bondage?'

Later, Mrs Mervyn said to her husband, with a shake of her head, 'I think he sees us as Israelites. It really is very strange.'

She did all she could to make him part of the community, inviting him on to her charity committees which organized parish jumble sales, raffles and fêtes, and it was because he'd offered his quarters as a storeroom that Ndbele acquired the great piles of old newspapers which were later to be so important to him.

The chief minister of Ndbele's independent homeland wrote an inquiring letter:

Dear Father,
Have you civilized them yet? I'll bet not! Those people are built to the old design. The only way you'll ever fix them is to scrap the lot and start rebuilding from the ground up. Take my word for it.

Yours encouragingly,
Gabriel Shushwe (Chief Minister)

Ndbele replied thanking the chief minister for his concern and saying that although he was completely at one with his people it was probably too soon to expect his people to have become one with him.

It was very shortly after this that there were delivered the two hammer blows which were to smash the last vestiges of Father O'Shea's hopes of having the black priest accepted as a normal member of the congregation. The trouble began when O'Shea placed Father Ndbele on what was known as the 'late list'. This was the stand-by roster for which priests volunteered and it meant they could be called out at any time of the day or night to administer the last rites to the dying; at least in practice, up until then, priests had volunteered but Father O'Shea was determined that the majority of these cases would be seen by the black priest. That way, he reasoned, his parishioners would come to see him merely as another priest whom they needed in this vital role as the bringer of relief and comfort and grace to the departing soul, and the prejudices against Ndbele would slowly disappear. A man who could treat you when you were dying, Father O'Shea reasoned, would surely be allowed to join the Catholic Men's Guild and the other powerful parish steering committees traditionally dominated by Boy Stockenstroom and his people. This plan had a most unforeseen and regrettable consequence. It led to the first of the two hammer blows which destroyed O'Shea's best hopes, namely death and the chemical toilet.

When the call came for extreme unction it seemed to Father O'Shea to have a singular appropriateness and it showed once again the mysterious ways in which God moved, for it represented a chance of revealing, more graphically than any sermon, that in desperate situations the human soul cries out to its priest for consolation, regardless of his skin colour.

The distraught and dishevelled caller was Jeff Craskil, Stockenstroom's willing lieutenant in the anti-Ndbele brigade, frantic with worry and lack of sleep, a biscuit-coloured duffle coat pulled hastily over his striped pyjamas which flapped showing bony ankles and black shoes with trailing laces. His mother was sinking fast and the priest would have to hurry. He had no time left to argue when he was presented with Father Ndbele carrying his little leather bag with the holy oil and sacred viaticum, though it must be said he managed through white lips to express the hope that his poor mother would not be too startled at finding what he called a 'strange priest' in the house. She was after all one of the old school, he said with a significant look at Father O'Shea, if he knew what that meant. Father O'Shea knew what it meant but chose not to reply. Instead he simply looked at his watch and Craskil fled into the night with Ndbele in tow.

The old lady lay on a great bed with a carved headboard of yellow oak in whose high polish were reflected the stacked pillows propping her and her thin grey hair. Her mouth was open and she breathed in short and sharp, tiny breaths and there was a little sweat on her lip. The doctor was packing up and told Ndbele that there was nothing more he could do, that she had had moments of lucidity throughout the evening but it was unlikely that she would say anything to him now. Jeff Craskil went with the doctor when he left the room and Ndbele closed the door and went and sat down by the bed. There was no response when he whispered her name. It was too late to hear her confession and she was in no condition to receive holy communion. Taking the little bottle of holy oil from his bag and a swab of cotton wool he began to anoint her. This was his first death and seeing old Mrs Craskil so peaceful Ndbele was relieved, there was something reassuring, almost touching, about the gentle departure. Dabbing the oil on her forehead and whispering a general absolution he was astonished to see her eyes open wide, as if his touch had revived her; clear and grey they focused on him.

Disconcerted he sat down on the chair by her side. His attempt to administer extreme unction, the viaticum, the consolation to speed the departing soul on its way, appeared to have had the opposite effect. Mrs Craskil was very much alive, indeed she appeared to be trying to sit up in the bed.

'Well Thomas – what's this I find? Sitting down on the job?' Her voice was strong, clear and demanding. A trace of holy chrism he'd left on her forehead gleamed at him. To his horror she continued to struggle up in bed until she lay propped on one elbow. 'Well, go on,' she commanded. 'Don't think because I'm sick I can't keep an eye on you.' She glared at him.

Ndbele was nonplussed, but only momentarily. Looking down he saw he was still holding the swab of cotton wool and the bottle of oil.

'Well get on with it, boy.'

Ndbele walked over to the corner, dabbed a little oil on the cotton wool and began polishing the large chest of drawers, conscious that she was watching him closely.

'And when you've finished, Thomas, I want to see my face in those drawers, shining like the sun.' With a long sigh she lay back on the pillows.

Ndbele kept his head down, concentrating on his work. He was pleased that Chief Gabriel Shushwe couldn't see him now. He was pleased no one could see him now. However, what course was open to him but to respect the wishes of the dying? He blew on the fine grain of the wood and rubbed again. The shine was coming up beautifully. He went on polishing until he was quite sure that the feeble breathing in the big bed had ceased.

Outside the room Jeff Craskil sat in a chair, head bowed, white-faced and weeping softly, his toe-caps touching beneath his pyjama trousers, the laces trailing. Beside him stood another, bigger man in electric blue flannels and a white open-necked shirt through which the chest hairs prickled like black needles. He had a red angry neck and scrubby hair, both of which he was rubbing angrily with a large square hand.

Craskil turned his brown eyes upward in a sad inquiring glance at Ndbele, who shook his head. Making an effort to control himself Craskil indicated the big man. 'This here is my mother's relation from Uitenhage. He's been travelling all night to be here before – he was devoted to her.'

The relation from Uitenhage barely glanced at Ndbele.

'Can I go in now? Can I see her?'

'Mrs Craskil has passed away,' Ndbele said softly. 'It was very peaceful. I think she was happy at the end.'

Jeff Craskil sighed deeply, he had been preparing himself for this.

'Why don't you go in and see your grannie now?' Ndbele suggested kindly to the relation from Uitenhage.

'Strictly speaking, she's not really his grannie, it's a distant relationship. But he was devoted to her,' Craskil said.

The big man went over to Craskil and began banging him on the chest. 'What's this black chappie got to do with anything?'

'He's a priest.' Craskil caught the big man's fist in his hands and patted it reassuringly. 'Perhaps we should go in and see her now.'

The relation from Uitenhage stood there in what were no doubt his best electric blue flannels and his white open-necked shirt through which even more chest hairs now pricked like black needles and out of which his red angry neck massively jutted, and leaving his fist in Craskil's grasp, he reached up with his free hand and rubbed angrily at his scrubby hair in furious confusion. 'What's there to see? She's gone. After travelling hundreds of miles to see her I arrive to find some bloody native has beaten me to it.'

'I was glad to give her what comfort I could,' Ndbele said modestly. 'The place of the priest at such times is with his people.'

The big man withdrew his fist from Craskil's consoling clasp and with it hit Ndbele in the face. 'You haven't got no people here!' cried the grief-stricken relative. 'To think she closed her eyes on that face . . .'

Craskil helped Ndbele to his feet. 'He was devoted to her. I did warn you.'

'She died peacefully. I can promise you that, sir.'

'Peacefully! I'll give you peace!' The big man hit Ndbele again in the face.

'And he's not a Catholic. That's the problem,' said Craskil.

Now this attack on Father Ndbele presented the parish priest, Father O'Shea, with considerable problems. He could not be seen to be in any way overlooking or condoning the assault on one of his priests engaged on a mission of mercy. He interviewed Jeff Craskil and found the man distinctly unhelpful. There was the question of his relation's deep devotion to old Mrs Craskil, there was in addition the fact that he had told Ndbele that the man was regrettably not a Catholic, and perhaps most importantly there was that fact that his relation did after all come from Uitenhage and people there, he put it to Father O'Shea, were probably most unused to the sight of African men emerging from the bedrooms of cherished family members late at night. Father O'Shea rejected all of these explanations and roundly condemned the attack on one of his priests. 'A priest is God's man on earth,' he told Craskil fiercely. Craskil, angered by what seemed to him an unjustified attack, retorted that if Father believed that, Father would believe anything.

Sam Mervyn and his wife, Reynolds, O'Hara and Old Valenti announced that they would encourage Ndbele to sue the relation from Uitenhage, that they would find a lawyer and pay his costs, that this was an issue on which it was vital to take a stand. Father O'Shea found himself in a dilemma. He did not feel that he could for a moment allow anyone to believe that he thought of the attack as anything other than outrageous, stupid and impious. On the other hand he recoiled from the vision of a court case, of members of the parish, of the warring political factions parading through the witness box and, inevitably, across the back pages of the Sunday papers.

It was Ndbele himself who got Father O'Shea off the hook. He declared that on the one hand the attack by the relation from Uitenhage was a most serious assault not least because, whether Catholic or not, the man had laid violent hands on God's anointed. On the other hand, there was the question of the man's grief, and a grief-stricken man is not responsible for his actions. And certainly he had no intention whatsoever of pressing charges. In fact he rather thought he may have provoked the relation from Uitenhage. On reflection he had decided that in his behaviour on the night in question there was clearly a certain element of provocation.

Father O'Shea rubbed his forehead disbelievingly. 'You're asking me to accept that you were in some way responsible for this primitive attack?'

Ndbele nodded.

'But how? What did you do?'

Ndbele fingered his bruised cheekbone and rolled his eyes reflectively. 'After he had hit me the first time and I got up again I think it was quite clearly in my mind as I faced him that what I intended was to turn the other cheek.'

Curiously enough when this news got around, both camps, though for their own reasons, were left equally aghast; Stockenstroom's side at the unbelievable arrogance this attitude implied, and Sam Mervyn's supporters at what they regarded as Ndbele's regrettable failure to seize this opportunity to take a white bully to court and throw the book at him. And these reactions, different though they were, had the inevitable effect of drawing, for the very first time, everyone in the parish more closely together. For the first time all of them, irrespective of their political opinions, could be seen to have reservations about Ndbele.

It was soon after this that Father O'Shea, having come secretly and regretfully to recognize Ndbele's increasingly ambivalent status in the parish, transferred him from the 'late list' to the charitable functions which abounded in the parish, those activities he and his fellow priests amongst themselves referred to as 'the social round', various committees, mostly comprising well-meaning women, which organized jumble sales, Sunday night dances, badminton, amateur dramatics, bring-and-buy sales, white elephant stalls, cake-and-candy sales. It was in this supporting role that Ndbele had first begun to solicit, collect and store in his own room considerable supplies of old newspapers. It was also about this time that, looking back, a change might have been discerned in Ndbele. For the first time instead of being merely delegated or seconded to various duties, the little priest chose to involve himself in something of his own.

He began to take an interest in the big garden, acres of wilderness, an overgrown and derelict thicket of confusion stretching from the west wall of the church to the bordering firs. He was soon a familiar sight stumping through the undergrowth, wearing an old straw hat, his cassock hitched up into his belt, his sleeves rolled well past the elbows and sweat glinting on his forehead, tending the bougainvillaea or pruning the roses. He was successful at unblocking and then carefully restocking the fish pond. He excelled at cutting back the ivy, scything the knee-high, yellow-brown grass, amidst the summer paradise of singing, stinging, buzzing insect life, uprooting the black-jacks, tidying the cypress trees and lopping dead branches from the firs.

He also worked very successfully with the women on

the committees, a fact which O'Shea found pleasing though slightly disturbing. The women returned his enthusiasm by encouraging him in his work in the garden, Mrs Mervyn declaring that it was as if he found in this a way of taking root, and even Mrs Stockenstroom remarked that perhaps Father Ndbele was giving them all an object lesson in the truth that equality could not be enforced, that a man had to make his own choice, that he had to win acceptance in the community and perhaps Father Ndbele, slaving in the garden, was getting back to basics, quite literally grounding himself in their midst.

The men saw it rather differently. Sam Mervyn said quite frankly that much as the garden needed attention he couldn't see the good of a priest burying himself in his own backyard when his real function was the cure of souls, and Stockenstroom the builder, in a mood of uncharacteristic and rather menacing reflection, wondered if it was not perhaps merely that the new priest had found his own level. Father O'Shea began doubting, despite the bishop's assurances, that Ndbele represented a determination by holy mother Church to embrace its responsibilities in South Africa and this question was further clouded by another which he did not like even to admit though it knocked around in the back of his head with worrying frequency, and it was this: if indeed Ndbele was a sign, was he the precise sign Our Lord had quite intended?

The connection, the fatal connection as it proved, between Ndbele's collection of old newspapers and his work in the garden may never have occurred had it not been for the incident at the annual Easter fête when the second of the hammer blows fell.

Ndbele was becoming increasingly noted for his work on the committees which comprised the social round, even if the popularity he was beginning to win was unavoidably confined to that minority of active women who organized these events. It was a start, the more optimistic said and even the pessimists had to agree that it was better than nothing. The annual Easter fête was held on the playing fields of a nearby school where a huge pink and white marquee was pitched, surrounded by several subsidiary tents housing a rich variety of stalls, tea and tombola, white elephant, jumble, darts and bingo. The priests came of course, everyone came: it was the premier fundraising event of the year. Ndbele had been there since early morning. He had helped to put up the tents and he had judged the homemade jams with what everybody agreed had been great delicacy and aplomb. They say he won a small bottle of shampoo on the tombola stand, lost a few pennies at darts and Craskil's young daughter had brought him a cup of tea, which everyone thought was a good omen and hinted at, some felt, a growing air of acceptance of the little black priest.

It was one of those perfect afternoons when the clean, delightful sunshine of an African autumn lay shining on the thick, rugged grass of the playing fields. Perhaps after all it was true that different races could accommodate each other, perhaps this was the beginning. Perhaps. Sadly, the hopes for better relations, hopes which had taken such a knock with the death of old Mrs Craskil, were to be blasted entirely by the affair of the chemical toilet.

Like everything else that day at the fête, the chemical toilet was inside a tent. It was a very small tent, rectangular, of faded green canvas shaped rather like a telephone kiosk and it came complete with a canvas door which was shut by clicking home the large brass press studs which ran down the edge. The builder Stockenstroom was first in the queue outside the little tent, behind him stood Sam

Mervyn and behind him Jeff Craskil. The sun was dropping lower in the sky and the queue threw lengthening black shadows on the green grass, a soft crisp breeze blew and an air of serenity touched the waiting men, that curious spirit of geniality which has a way of coming up on people unexpectedly in Africa. They feel the pleasantness of the late afternoon sun on their necks, raise their eyes to a high blue heaven and feel that all they survey, all the work of their hands, has been well done. It is a feeling of togetherness, of camaraderie, which leads respectable middle-aged women to take off their shoes in public places and sit down on the grass and takes men from silent reflection, scuffing a toe absent-mindedly in the turf, to rowdy sessions in hotel bars in the first glow of sunset. The setting sun is an event in Africa. Sundown unlocks the doors. The sun goes out like a lion and in the faint glow remaining an inexplicable and yet somehow comforting pride springs up in the hearts of white people particularly, leading women to gossip and men to brood and everyone thereafter to the drinks trolley and the hotel bar and the cocktail cabinet there to set the seal on their togetherness before the night closes in.

This mood of geniality was upon Stockenstroom who stood like a sentry, his feet slightly apart, his arms behind his back, shifting his weight from one foot to the other, patiently waiting. And he was very patient. He pointed out to Sam Mervyn, to whom he had not been talking for some weeks, that some wag had gone and chalked 'Please knock' on the canvas door. They both laughed and Mervyn turned and told Jeff Craskil. And eventually Stockenstroom at Sam Mervyn's urging politely asked the occupant of the toilet to hurry things along. The voice that replied in clear, unemotional terms shocked the waiting men, it was so unexpected. In a voice much louder than was needed to carry through the thin canvas Ndbele insisted that people would simply have to wait until he was finished. To his credit, Stockenstroom did as he was told. He waited, gouging at the back of his neck furiously with his stubby fingers, but waiting none the less. Mervyn, who was so very embarrassed, as he told his wife later, he didn't know where to put his face, whistled tunelessly. Craskil openly sneered. A few minutes later Stockenstroom, making an effort to keep his voice under control, once again asked the occupant of the tent to get a move on. The queue recoiled when the voice declared it impossible to hurry a call of nature. Deep and low somewhere inside him a reverberating note, or perhaps a croak so low, so frog-like, rose up in the builder and bubbled from his lips.

'I'll give you a call of nature!' he shrieked and opening his big arms he ran at the tent as if to embrace it, dragged it off its four wooden feet in his great bear hug and tossed it aside. 'When I say out, I mean out! You cheeky black devil!'

The tent toilet demolished at a stroke lay in a jumble of struts and canvas and there presented to the sight of the whole world was a spectacle which, as Father O'Shea said afterwards, was to cause scandal, humiliation and deep anguish to Father Ndbele himself and to all who saw it, and it is doubtful that there was anyone on that field who didn't see it. A spectacle at once brutal and farcical, the sight of Father Ndbele, with his cassock hitched to his waist and underpants around his ankles, sitting on the chemical toilet in the middle of the fête. A woman screamed, several children cried, Stockenstroom simply stood there smacking his hands together in a workmanlike way, Sam Mervyn turned his back, even Craskil stared at the passing crowd. Only Ndbele moved, in a fluid movement he reached down and then stood, his cassock safely in place swung at his ankles; his composure was astonishing and the few who could bring themselves to watch said he left the ground with the casual, natural air they found eerie and disturbing. Stockenstroom, of course, tried to say later that he would have behaved in the same way whoever it had been in the toilet, to anyone who had spoken to him in that fashion. But he wasn't believed and Father O'Shea ordered him off the church premises, removed him from his committees, struck him from the parish roll. But the damage was done.

Reaction in the parish was strange and not at all what O'Shea had expected. He got the impression, in fact he got the distinct impression, that while everybody had been extremely embarrassed by what had happened at the fête, nobody really seemed to feel that what Stockenstroom had done was reprehensible; to his alarm he sensed that people thought it was understandable and in fact if anyone was to blame for the incident it had been Ndbele, who by allowing himself to be exposed in the way he had been shattered the mood of golden geniality in which the day was ending. People held it against him, there was no doubt of that, it was almost as if they felt that he had been responsible for the attack and the builder Stockenstroom merely his unwitting victim.

Ndbele's humiliating appearance had disturbed the afternoon, it had offended the guests and his eerily dignified exit seemed positively to have enraged all who had seen it. Mrs Ada Stockenstroom's comment was typical: 'It's being a native that does it. You know what I mean.' At this point she would look hard at her hearers. 'It's being a native,' she would add again. She had their attention and was certain of their understanding. 'It's being used to being in the veld. They can just come and go there. They use the grass. For them it's natural.'

Father Ndbele returned to his garden. Parish work was no longer an issue for him. He was off the late list, he was off the social round and he spent a great deal of time carrying large white enamel basins of water into his bedroom. Father O'Shea said nothing, he was merely grateful that Ndbele seemed so fully occupied. Besides he could think of nothing to say.

One morning the reasons for the work Ndbele was doing in his room became apparent; the first of the figures appeared in the garden. It stood beneath an olive tree and was discovered by some altar boys on their way to serve the early morning mass. He was a policeman. He stood on one leg beneath the olive tree, his uniform was perfect in every detail, the peaked khaki cap, the khaki shorts, the Sam Browne over the smart russet tunic, the belt, the revolver in its holster and the handcuffs gleaming beside the truncheon dangling from its hip thong, thick brown woollen socks and the brown shoes with toe-caps boned and gleaming, though slightly misty with the early morning condensation, a pirouetting figure, one leg thrown out behind it, hands reaching into the air, head tilted back and the shadow from the cap peak shortening as the sun rose on the pallid papier-mâché features, carefully modelled and hand painted, a policeman rearing on one leg and reaching out his arms in the early morning sunshine, the first of Ndbele's people. The next morning a second figure appeared, correct in every detail from cap to toe and linking his arm in his fellow's, the pair flung their heads and feet and arms in a spirited, high-kicking dance.

The dancing policemen were the first of a set of monumental figures which were soon to occupy every corner of the garden. There followed these others: Angels Digging, a winged working party who had already scooped away in the night a great hollow of earth or a swimming pool or a ditch or even perhaps a grave, and now stood leaning on their spades and contemplating their handiwork, their great wings arching behind them, the papier-mâché thickly sprinkled with gold glitter. A working party of six. Next came the Dying Priest Attended by a Child who lay on a stretcher of twigs beneath an old army-issue blanket. His hands folded piously on his chest, the face white and staring, perhaps he was already dead, perhaps he did not see the child who had stopped beside him, holding a hoop and stick, the hoop an old bicycle wheel, the sort you saw small children driving with long wire whips in any African village, and was clearly intended as some reference to the Christ child. The priest's hair had been contrived with strips of old brown sacking and had a coarse and desperate look to it and it was with a terrible shock that Father O'Shea recognized that the features were modelled on his own. A moment's inspection showed him that the two dancing policemen had the faces of Stockenstroom and Sam Mervyn, Jeff Craskil was to be found among the angels digging as was the effigy of old Colonel Pienaar.

It did not take long thereafter to realize that what Ndbele was doing with his figures was to replace in so far as that was possible the entire parish with the population in his garden. Each day there was something new, Three Apostles Racing, Christ Wrestling a Lion in which a huge naked Christ with the face of the bishop wrestled an ungainly and rather lumpy lion. Ndbele never aimed at close realism, except in the modelling of the faces which was astonishingly done, but for the rest he aimed for force and movement, modelling his undependable and inflexible chosen medium of papier-mâché on to frames of compressed chicken wire. His last great work, a tableau of no less than sixteen figures, the Virgin Attended by her

Golfers, took him almost three months to build and showed the Virgin upon a rock, rather reminiscent of the Little Mermaid, receiving a deputation of golfers, the first of whom kneels before her presenting a symbolic putter while the other golfers bring up the rear, tired and travel-stained, evidently after a long pilgrimage. The Virgin's face was that of Mrs Mervyn.

Ndbele wrote to his chief about this time:

Esteemed Sir,
My prayers have been answered. Praise be the Lord. He has allowed his servant to come among His people at last! My ambition is to lead them out of the bondage in which I have found them, to lead them home to the land of their Fathers. Pray for me, Beloved Chief. Ask that my prayers are answered.

Father O'Shea asked him, 'Are these your people?'

'Your own lips have said it.' Ndbele held up two fingers pressed tightly together. 'Bone of my bone, blood of my blood. I will not allow one hair of their heads to be harmed.'

Father O'Shea nodded, he seemed to approve of these sentiments. 'Well in that case what are you going to do when it rains?'

The rain of course played havoc with the figures, they dissolved, they floated, old headlines appeared on their foreheads. Father Ndbele was almost equal to the task and he began building shelters, using any material he could find, old cardboard boxes, corrugated iron, plastic sheeting; he built lean-to's, porticos, alcoves, grottoes and tents to house his people and to keep them from the rain. Before long it seemed as if an entire shanty town had sprung up beside the quiet west wall of the church.

Something had to be done. This was a sad necessity, or perhaps a kindness. Some of the women, reminded of their cordial relations with Father Ndbele, suggested that it was clear that things simply could not go on, that the church now stood beside a slum, a township, a location full of strangely pallid natives, sleeping, standing, dancing, living and dying in shanties and lean-to's.

The attention of the municipal planning department might be drawn, it was suggested, to the obvious contravention of the zoning laws, the building regulations and the environmental provisions for the neighbourhood. However, this presented difficulties because the order, if the order was to be made against a new town, must demand the removal of Ndbele's shanties without in any way threatening the rest of church property and this was always a very delicate matter since the Catholic Church existed uneasily beneath the hostile scrutiny of a Calvinist Nationalist government opposed to the Church of Rome, commonly referred to as the Roman Danger. Once the authorities had been appealed to, the danger was, O'Shea knew, that he might find himself facing an artillery barrage fired by a government gunner who might not be unhappy at the thought of knocking out more acres of church property than simply the little patch populated by Ndbele's people. It was not even certain that the government inspectors could be expected to act at all, since they may have preferred to sit back and enjoy Father O'Shea's discomfiture and his bishop's dismay at the way in which their plans had gone awry. If the appropriate authorities were to be approached, they must be diplomatically sounded out as to ways in which the business could be accomplished, how the necessary injunction was to be shaped, and then aimed so as to hit only that excrescence of canvas, cardboard, cheap matchwood and old sacking which now disfigured the formerly fair west wall of the parish church, occupying what had been the garden stretching from the box hedge to the fir trees marking the border, a pleasant if rather bedraggled spot before it had been colonized or, as some said, squatted, by the rag-tag assembly of the pious and profane creatures who had become known as Ndbele's people.

Father O'Shea called a meeting of the parish council knowing as he did so what their answer was likely to be and so felt little surprise and a keen regret when they told him that the only man with the necessary connections among municipal planning officials and the know-how of the building trade as well as the right political credentials was the builder Stockenstroom; even the Mervyns with their liberal attachments felt the undeniable logic of this. Jeff Craskil announced himself as ready to act as intermediary between the council and its former chairman and said firmly that he knew old Stockenstroom was far too decent a chap to bear any grudges.

Stockenstroom responded promptly to the suggestion that he approach the municipality and in a letter to Father O'Shea said that the job was a difficult one and one which would require him to bring all his influence to bear on his friends in the Planning Department, but declaring himself warmed by the confidence of the parish council and promising to do whatever he could to help, particularly in view of what he liked to think of as his long association with the council. The significance of these last words was not lost on the committee. The job was to be done on the clear understanding that if successful Stockenstroom was to find himself gratefully reinstated as a full member of the congregation, his reward would be a return to the fold. Jeff Craskil was heard to remark that he understood now why there was more joy in heaven over the single sheep that is lost and found than over the ninety-nine that had been saved all along. Sam Mervyn retorted that he did not see the comparison at all and that Stockenstroom, in his opinion, was more wolf than sheep, and Father O'Shea moved quickly to hush this bickering.

He telephoned Chief Shushwe to prepare him for things to come: 'We thought, that is the bishop and I, that a visit home might be in order. We think it may help.'

'Help who?' The chief was brusque. 'I need a priest here like I need rabies. He went over to you guys because we thought you needed help. He was supposed to spread a little light among the heathen. Mind you I thought it was a mistake at the time. You guys are damned incorrigible, there's no curing you. But the little fellow is so enthusiastic. He is better than you deserve and you know it. I just hope you treated him decently. What's he going to do back in the bush all alone? Got no fancy church here.'

'He is not exactly alone.'

The chief shrieked. 'Not alone? You mean he's got company? You've got to be crazy, Father, have you any idea where I'm speaking from? My so-called independent country is a denuded, eroded, poverty-stricken dustbowl. Nothing much grows here, nothing much lives, and very few of us eat, and you're planning to send Ndbele back here with a party?'

'It is not so much of a party as a following.'

'What does it matter? It's still mouths and they will want feeding.'

'I think, Chief Shushwe, you will find these people far from demanding.'

'How did he get these people? Is he some sort of a guru where you live – little Ndbele? Where do they come from?'

'They sort of sprang up,' O'Shea said uneasily.

'Jesus, what do you mean? Has the boy been breeding in captivity?'

'We will lay on a form of transport, rely on us.' O'Shea promised desperately and hung up.

Ndbele stared at the injunction tightly packed with numbered regulations and decrees forbidding the erection of unscheduled, unplanned, illegal dwellings, domiciles, cottages, garages, mobile homes, car ports and all other forms of walled and/or roofed habitations . . .

'What does this mean?' he appealed to O'Shea.

'It has nothing to do with the Church. I am very sorry. The government say they will come with bulldozers and break all of your people.'

The little priest stood erect. 'Then I will lie down in the path of the bulldozers. People have done so before. The government are always coming with their bulldozers, we are not afraid.'

'Then you must know that the government and its bulldozers always win. They will lay flat this place and all your people and then will pick up the pieces and throw them on the rubbish heap.'

The little black priest's agonized silence testified to the truth of these remarks.

O'Shea thrust home the advantage. 'But, on the other hand, if they were to be taken to a place of safety . . .'

Ndbele raised anxious eyes. 'You know of such a place?'

O'Shea inclined his head. 'The homeland. The land of your fathers.'

'That is possible, but it would not be home to my people.'

'Not home, but a place to rest for a while. A place for them to lay their heads.'

Ndbele swung and faced north and stared with narrowed eyes at the distant horizon. After a long moment he said, 'It would be a refuge. It might seem a wilderness but at least they will be safe for a time. They could gather their strength for the journey into the land promised.' He wheeled suddenly on O'Shea. 'You would not try to stop us leaving?'

Father O'Shea smiled gently. 'Stop you? Why should I stop you? I am not Pharaoh. No, I shall not stop you. In fact I intend to arrange your transport.'

The day on which Ndbele and his people departed the parish was long remembered. Everyone turned up with the exception of Stockenstroom who, it was generally agreed, at his moment of triumph showed surprising tact in staying away.

The transport arrived promptly, three one-ton lorries, leased with parish funds from Moosa who hawked fruit and vegetables around the neighbourhood, rapidly rusting old lorries with open sides, and each with its scaffolding of steel poles on which from Monday to Saturday were hung Moosa's fruit and vegetables and sheaves of brown paper packets pierced on brass hooks now sliding musically along the rails at the slightest touch.

Everybody pitched in with a will that day. Supervised by Father O'Shea in a floppy khaki hat with a green brim, they rallied around the frantic figure of Ndbele whose energy was astounding, who was everywhere at once, admonishing, cajoling, thanking his helpers, whispering to his people, tenderly seeing to their comfort and welfare, as they were one by one taken from the garden and loaded aboard the lorries. The three Indian drivers were bossed by a rather haughty youth, a cousin of Moosa called Farum, and none of them lent a hand but instead sat on the bumper of the leading lorry, in what shade they could find, and told long vivacious stories to each other interspersed with peals of high-pitched laughter.

The figures presented many problems and it was hot

and delicate work lifting them over the tail gates and lashing them gently and firmly into place using the overhead rails and their jingling hooks for extra security. The policemen presented a particularly awkward problem with their flinging limbs for it was difficult to know how they could be secured without running the risk of a sudden jolt tearing off an arm or a leg. Eventually Mrs Mervyn suggested that they might be lashed together for added support and so they were secured, waist to waist first, and then tied to the corner posts. The dying priest had a tendency to slide about since Ndbele insisted that the old man was too ill to leave his bed and must be laid flat. Bracing him seemed impossible until Craskil, who had once been in the navy, hit on a brilliant solution and fashioned a hammock from an old blanket, and with this they slung the priest from the top bars of the lorry like a sleeping sailor. The Digging Angels filled almost the entire lorry themselves because of the great expanse of their feathery wings which flaked easily and so they had to be laid face down and all one saw of them from the road were the tips of their wings, quivering feathers shaking like a field full of shuttlecocks in the breeze. Lastly the houses, homes, lean-to's and shanties had also to be carefully taken down, numbered and stacked. It was late afternoon before the job was complete, the child with his hoop was now in place, the makeshift clubs borne by the golfers who tended the Virgin had been collected, numbered and wrapped in sacking. The garden was at last empty, the lorries loaded and the convoy ready to roll. The driver, Guram, heaved himself up into the driving seat of the leading vehicle. Ndbele clambered up onto a pile of corrugated iron on the last lorry. Craskil banged the leading lorry on the tail gate and then to a cheer of farewells Ndbele's people set off on the long road north.

The last glimpse Father O'Shea and his little band of helpers had of the convoy was of the dancing policemen, lashed trunk to trunk, oddly, eerily, intimately interwoven, swinging in their tight, roped embrace and then the tiny figure of Father Ndbele perched on his pile of corrugated iron with his knees drawn up to his chin and his face pointed to the north.

Chief Gabriel Shushwe sat in his office in a beehive-shaped building which echoed the style of the native huts outside but in his case was built of a bright and scratchy yellow-faced brick. Through the windows he could see the three lorries piled with their improbable cargo, and the three Indian drivers sitting on the front bumper. Ndbele stood before him looking around with big eyes.

'Okay, baby,' Shushwe commanded, 'spill.' With growing impatience he watched Ndbele glancing around his office, saw him staring at the huge teak desk and the armchairs, at the venetian blinds covering the windows, at the red baked earth beyond the blinds and the scruffy, dusty little fowls darting about, the swollen-bellied children in the doorways of the mud huts. Chief Gabriel felt a pang of something he hoped wasn't guilt. 'Don't knock it until you've tried it, right?' he instructed the priest. 'We're not here to talk about my position anyway. What did I send you out into the white world for, if not to teach those bastards a lesson? You were my assegai, remember? Tipped with tungsten. I expected you to punish them, to make them suffer. I wasn't sure if you'd manage it, mind you, but that was the general idea. I did not expect you to turn up here one day with a lorryload of ghouls tied up with ropes and three Asian drivers. God dammit, man, you were sent out there to throw pepper into the eyes of the white racists, not to start your own tribe!'

Ndbele gave him a proud look. 'A man cannot choose his own destiny.'

Gabriel stared out of the window and thought of America, of his happy days at Penn State University. Sunlight on the Delaware. A girl called Sheena. Outside his window he saw a woman, baby strapped on her back, tending a row of mealies, hacking the iron ground with an old hoe. 'You're telling me, boy,' he said feelingly.

Chief Gabriel slept on the problem. But in the praise-songs of his tribe it is related that that night he dreamed, though this was never confirmed. However, in the morning he spoke urgently to Ndbele who had slept the night on the back of a lorry and he said nothing at all to the three Indian drivers who were by this time angry, hungry and impatient. His words were prophetic: 'This is thin country, there's no place for you here.'

When Ndbele asked where he should go, the chief's reply was to climb up into the cab of the leading lorry and to order Guram to drive.

They drove along the new, metalled road leading to the casino, they drove through the huge car parks where the sun shone liquid on a thousand Japanese sedans and they drove through the serried ranks of tourist buses, past the tennis courts, past the great gate with its motif of animal horns marking the entrance to the game reserve and stopped in front of the great glass doors that led into the foyer of the new casino.

Chief Gabriel Shushwe's first words to the entrepreneur Karam are legend: 'Be of good cheer, baby,' he said, 'a holy man has come amongst you.'

Karam swore. He tore his shirt in his rage. It did no good.

The full-sized rugby field was chosen as the best site. The pavilion and sprinkler system ensured that there would be a supply of running water. Soon that green and luxuriant patch of grass between the touch-lines took on a more homely aspect as Ndbele began rebuilding the shelters.

'It came to me,' Chief Shushwe told Karam, 'that what this boy needed was a promised land and you're the nearest thing to it.'

'I won't support these people,' Karam warned.

'They're your employees now. On contract,' Shushwe warned.

'Jesus wept!' the Lebanese yelled.

'And you better cut out that sort of talk right now. They're holy.'

Karam ripped aside the tattered shred of his shirt to expose his chest. 'Cut my heart out while you're about it. Drink my blood!'

'I don't want nothing myself,' Shushwe said seriously, 'but if you've got any morsels you could spare I'm sure Father Ndbele would be damn grateful.'

Ndbele showed no gratitude to the entrepreneur in the Sunday sermons he preached to his people comparing him to a modern pharaoh holding his tribe in bondage, this to the great amusement of the curious gamblers, who as news spread would wander down from the casino for a breath of fresh air, marvel at the dignity of the tribe camped among the bits of tarpaulin, canvas, flapping blankets and corrugated iron and inspect with growing awe the figures ranged across the rugby field: dancing policemen and dying priest, digging angels and the Virgin's faithful golfers and all the holy company of Ndbele's people, now grown to a small city full of many more strange white folk, apostles with microscopes, Magdalene laughing and a St Paul, who had the face of the relation from Uitenhage, cycling. And although Ndbele might have charged something for this casual viewing he never did so; all he expected in return for the guided tours he offered and his free sermons, was a sympathetic ear into which he would pour with icy and sardonic range the story of how his people had been dispossessed and driven from their land, how they had been forced into exile and how they would endure and one day return. 'Return', he said, lifting his fist above his head, 'driving all before them.'

Whatever Happened to Vilakazi?

All I know for sure is that he went missing sometime between the Saturday evening before Quinquagesima Sunday (which in that year, so clearly do I remember it, fell on the 3rd of March) and the following Wednesday, Ash Wednesday. In that dark, devouring time as the Church bares itself and makes ready for the chastisement of the Lenten days ahead my thoughts were turning, even more swiftly than usual, to the prospect of sudden death, about which there was a lot of seasonal talk in catechism lessons, and you were either like Billy Hendriks who, though he was also an altar server, called the whole thing a lot of bally tripe, or you were like Bastable who had been knocked down and killed earlier that year, shortly after he'd been to confession, and was held up as an example of a very lucky boy, or you were like me, secretly admiring Hendriks' nerve while expecting Bastable's fate, without his luck. As the reminders of mortality piled up that week, my fears grew, fatally drawing me into the church for a devotional visit on the Saturday evening after a game of badminton with Hendriks in the parish hall which he'd won despite the fact that he was so bad he held his racket in both hands and had only one stroke, a pushing shot beginning at his nose and ending at his knees.

It was in the darkened church through clasped fingers that I saw the strange figure at the altar rails. The sight dismayed and frightened me, it made me feel guilty and yet, helpless, so much so that when there was no sign of the boy on the Sunday morning around the parish gardens or the vestry door, I was actually rather relieved. But when there was still no sign of him by Wednesday I knew I had to do something, and besides too many of the other servers had noticed his disappearance to ignore it.

Even then I delayed until school was out; I might have gone after mass that morning. On Ash Wednesday it was customary for the entire school to make its way to the parish church where Father Besserman assisted by two priests carrying large white porcelain urns moved up and down the altar rails where nearly five hundred boys knelt piously with their fists kneading their closed eyes, breathing the smell of starch in the white altar cloth covering the rails, newly washed by Brother Musel, and felt the priest lightly sign with his thumb the fatal mark on their foreheads and heard the murmured reminder that man was dust and unto dust he would return. I felt Father Besserman's crisp touch, like footsteps on cinders magnified in my ears and heard his whispered Latin prophecy of my mortality, saw behind my eyelids the black draped bier in the aisle and the six tall candles of my own mass for the dead, now surely very near, and made my way back to my pew wrinkling my forehead gently in a reverent effort to feel the cross of ash Father Besserman had printed there.

I might have gone to see him after mass about the missing boy, but still I delayed. Maybe he'd turn up, I told myself, without much hope in my heart. For the rest of that day one tended to avert one's eyes from one's friends; it was hard to see them as condemned men. There was an unwritten law forbidding you to rub out your cross, you had to wait for the wind and your hair and the natural erasure of daily wear. Usually by early afternoon it was safe to begin looking your friends in the face again as by then usually only the ashy ghosts of crosses remained, dark smudges, wispy flakes caught in the eyebrows, and you breathed more easily, seeing your friends no longer as creatures marked for death but merely as boys with dirty foreheads.

After school I went to see Father Besserman because Hendriks and the others said that if I didn't they would and so I had no option, feeling dreadfully obliged to do so anyway since I knew more than any of them and the weight of my knowledge depressed and wearied me.

Father Besserman was pitiless in his kindly understanding: 'He was a stray and you can't make pets of such creatures. He has gone as he arrived – without our consent.'

'But he's a boy, Father. Something may have happened.'

He put his arm around my shoulders. 'To you he's a boy. To me he's a boy, maybe, but in fact he's really a man. Made strong by the street. Maybe he went back to his friends. His pack.'

He knew what I was thinking when he used that word because he said, 'If you like ask Brother Musel. He's good at keeping an eye on boys, not so?'

'Brother Musel didn't like him. Brother Musel threw stones at him.'

Father Besserman frowned but did not contradict me. 'All the more reason why maybe he is the last to see him, *ja*?'

Brother Musel looked after the altar boys and he looked after the rich garments in the vestry, the gorgeous copes picked out in their holy geometry of gold and silver thread; he folded and handled and watched over, too, the deep brown drawers and cupboards housing maniples and chasubles, the candlesticks, the supplies of hosts and the sacramental wine, the dully gleaming chalices; and he took in all the laundry that needed doing and washed and dried it down in his boiler room where he stoked the great furnace that fed the boiler. Square-headed, grizzled around the jaws, he was launderer, janitor, sacristan, master of the altar boys and general dogsbody to the superior fathers of the order. His face was deeply lined, remote and deceptively dreamy for he was not a gentle man. The broad capable hands, the great muscles got by shovelling coal and his capacity for continuous hard work were always noticeable. He had a habit of humming to himself. As you pulled on your black cassock and your white surplice on one side of the wooden panelling you could hear Brother Musel at work on the other, folding, hanging and tidying, humming above the clash of the big wooden hangers and the somehow deeply reassuring 'clock-clock' of the birettas as Brother Musel slid each winged black hat home into the deep shelf in the cupboard where the copes were hung.

The priests of our parish were a German order and had settled in the area some twenty years before and so escaped the war, which was just as well, Billy Hendriks liked to say, because some of them would have made first-grade SS material. What I think he meant by that was that the German priests were so superior, clearly and effortlessly superior, to the local Europeans, and the Africans were simply beneath their notice; they exuded a peculiar kind of confidence which none of us could hope to match; though everyone we knew had been bred also to feel superior, in our case I think it was more a question of struggling always not to feel inferior. We had no confidence, our confidence had been undermined early by the poison of racialism which we took in with our mother's milk and so, whereas a salutary sense of themselves came naturally to the German priests, it was something we had to fight for; there was for us nothing like a natural hierarchy, to us social structure was war. I remember Audrey Hiemstra trying to explain to Father Besserman why she objected to a suggestion by some deranged liberal member of the congregation that the brass plaques on the four final pews in the church marked 'Reserved', so designating them for the use of Africans only, should be removed and Africans be allowed to sit where they liked. Mrs Hiemstra objected to this idea because, frankly, she told Father Besserman she was not prepared to sit beside black people or to allow her daughter to do so and as for her husband, well, she shuddered to think how he would react if he found himself in coloured company, since, she reminded him, her husband was, frankly, a mine manager and quite capable of taking offence at the slightest look, gesture or, here she paused delicately, odour, and thrashing the offending African right then and there, place of worship or not, sorry as she was, frankly, to have to admit it. She added that, of course, she didn't expect Father Besserman to understand or share or approve of her attitude, and again, frankly, she didn't care whether he did or not, but he had to understand how 'her' people felt about these things. She was white, she was very sorry about that, but there it was and she didn't believe everyone was created equal or wanted to be, or would ever be, nor did any of her family or friends. In an effort to reassure her, Father Besserman told her that he felt he understood exactly what she meant, even though, as he would be the first to admit, he hadn't been born in Africa, but in fact he confessed very cordially to feeling exactly the same about the Poles . . . What this admission achieved was to underline Father Besserman's incapacity for understanding things the way we did – all the same she was grateful to him for making the effort. 'Father Besserman doesn't like the Poles, you know,' she would tell people loudly after Sunday morning mass and they would nod cheerfully without any idea of what she meant, gathering from her tone that the man was doing his best.

Father Besserman, the rector, had a shining pink dome of a head on a short pink neck, stout as a surgical collar; a fair, firm, almost genial man; certainly in comparison with Brother Musel he was radiant light and it was his benign neglect which allowed Vilakazi to stay on, to gradually attach himself to the church when the general consensus among the rest of the priests would have been to boot him back across the hedge through which he had slipped into the gutter from where he had come when Billy and I found him on our way to serve early morning mass. He was curled up under a loquat tree fast asleep. I don't think we'd ever seen a child asleep in the open air on a brisk Highveld morning. All he had on was a pair of shorts, a man's shirt too large for him and an old sports coat. I remember we stared at his bare feet, at hard-skinned scaly soles with dust in the cracks and were struck by the fact that he was about the same age as we were. We couldn't get over that. We knew what he was, of course, he was a *piccanin*, a scamp from the streets, a young beggar, the sort of fellow who touched you for pennies in town, who joined with others into tattered orchestras for Christmas, playing their penny whistles and their biscuit tin drums and their primitive basses made from tea chests, broomstick handles and a string to strum, when, since they were an ingredient in the annual seasonal spirit, they were regarded as picturesque, though for the rest of the time they were acknowledged to be an unsightly and irritating nuisance.

On that first morning when we came out of mass he was cleaning our bikes with the end of his shirt sleeve; when he saw us he stood back with a smile and a flourish and stuck out his hand. Billy Hendriks gave him a cigarette and the boy tucked it behind his ear.

'What's your name?'

The boy tapped his chest. 'Vilakazi.'

Brother Musel appeared on the sacristy steps and bawled at us to report to him on the double and to bring black mischief along. He marched us off holding the frightened boy by his thin neck and paraded us before a bemused Father Besserman who, probably because he wasn't at all sure what was expected of him and perhaps as an evidence of good faith pointed at the cigarette behind his ear and invited him to smoke, ordering Brother Musel to give the boy a light, which the sacristan grudgingly did from the giant box he carried in his pockets for lighting the boiler furnace. We watched Vilakazi inhaling gratefully, openly smoking in front of adults in a way we would never dare to have done and envying him a certain freedom though envy could not go very far, not with us standing in our coats and our gloves and Vilakazi in his torn pants and bare feet, nodding every so often and politely collecting the ash in his palm, appearing to listen intently while Father Besserman told him that he might not remain on church property and must leave immediately. The boy smiled and nodded heartily though I think all of us realized he didn't understand what he heard and then we all went out of the church gates and Brother Musel sternly pointed Vilakazi into the distance. We watched him walking away with his head slightly bowed. Brother Musel smacked his hands together with an air of satisfaction which seemed excessive.

That night he was back; Brother Musel had spotted him when he rose before dawn to light the boiler and charged after him with his shovel. Vilakazi had bolted and he hadn't been able to catch him. 'But I got close enough to hit the little devil with a good stone – here on the back.' He jabbed a thumb between his shoulder blades. There was something deeply shaming in the picture of big Brother Musel pursuing the boy through the garden and throwing stones at him that made us flinch and shiver and so when we came out of mass and found Vilakazi waiting for us, smiling as broadly as ever and seemingly none the worse for it, all of us were hugely relieved and I think it was then in effect that we decided though we said nothing about it, to defend him as far as that was possible, in a sense to adopt him.

Gradually it became known to all the priests and to all the congregation that Vilakazi inhabited the garden and this unspoken fact was accepted by everyone except Brother Musel. He showed his dissatisfaction in various ways. He became even more scrupulous about the cleanliness of our cassocks and surplices, about the security of the wine and the wafers, about the locks on the great oak doors of the vestment cupboard and he would stride into the vestry in the early morning smelling of cinders from the furnace and soap from the laundry, his face flushed with the flames and steam of the place and reach into the cupboards twitching our surplices on their wire hangers, testing for dirt and humming deeply up and down a scale as if trying to remember an old tune. He had the sense to realize that the rest of the community were on Vilakazi's side, feeling that if the boy had the strength to stick it out he should be allowed somehow to stay on. He didn't rage against him but he never let the matter rest.

'They travel in groups, these boys. Like stray dogs, in packs. You let one in and soon you'll have the whole pack sleeping in the garden. It was like that in the old days on my father's estate.'

'Our Father's house has many mansions, Brother Musel,' said Father Besserman with an inclination of his head towards us, reminding his sacristan that the altar boys present expected conversation among the priests to have a religious tone to it.

'We have only one garden,' Brother Musel pointed out reasonably. 'In my father's place we found one day a single badger. What harm could a single badger do? That's what we asked. Soon the garden was full of badgers.'

'A single boy is scarcely a garden full of badgers,' Father Besserman said, carefully amiable.

'In the end we had to gas them, those badgers. My father he kept many cows. The badgers were infecting the cows. They gave them tuberculosis.'

Vilakazi must have known how delicate his position was and he kept low though he was always there when we arrived to serve mass, or for Wednesday novena or the Sunday benediction, smiling as if we were old friends with never a care in the world, but too wise not to understand his difficult position. He wasn't content simply to stay in the garden, he worked at establishing himself there, he tried to turn himself into the gardener and he'd go around sweeping up the leaves and pulling weeds and generally keeping everything tidy though he had no tools. He pulled the weeds by hand and I'd seen him sweeping, using a handful of branches as a broom, or on the pathway even using his bare feet. We approved of this; if he was going to stay then he would have to look as if he belonged, for belonging, we knew, was very much a question of appearances. There was in the corner of the garden, down by the hedge and beneath the great fir trees, a pump house controlling the water supply, it was in this that Vilakazi took up residence. The place was damp and smelt of oil and trembled with the thudding engine, but he appropriated it and no one objected. His bed consisted of an old tennis net, doubled and redoubled on the floor: on the wall were colour photographs torn from old magazines showing obscure South American rugby teams, all red shirts and big grins and folded arms, an old pair of bicycle handlebars he'd found somewhere and hung like chromium antlers on the wall, and a picture of a priest in his glory, dazzling in a crimson cope shot with silver thread, scalloped, embellished and glowing; this picture of the priest gave us an insight into what fascinated him about us because it was clear that even in our plain black and white cassocks and surplices we beguiled him and he loved nothing more than to take the edging of lace on the cuff between his fingers and rub it gently against his cheek talking in his language which we didn't understand.

I'd like to say that we got to know him well and, at a level below conversation, perhaps we did but his English never got any better and he never put on weight, darting through the bushes like the stray Musel said he was, scraggy, easily scared, endlessly cheerful, always begging for a cigarette and never looking much other than the little guy Hendriks and I had found asleep under the loquat tree. We brought him clothes, blankets and food, sometimes money and often cigarettes. I think we saw these gifts as our only weapons, outward signs and even warnings to Musel that we watched over Vilakazi.

On the Saturday evening before Quinquagesima Sunday I paid a visit to the church after playing a game of badminton with Hendriks in the parish hall next door and which I'd lost unnecessarily. My nerves were especially ragged. The nights that last week had been bad for this was the time I was going to sleep convinced that each night was my last, that I'd choke, or my heart would stop, or a vein would burst inside my head. I was quite convinced, or at least one part of me was convinced, and another part of me prayed wildly that the fate might be lifted from me, while yet a third part of me stood somewhat aside and watched sceptically to see what was going to happen, judging that while I was able to go on talking there must still be life in me and if I kept on talking long enough death might be slipped. I was praying almost constantly at the time, making visits to the church on every possible occasion and on the Saturday evening I threw myself down on my knees in the porch and prayed. The church was in darkness but the red light burning continuously before the tabernacle threw a glow across the altar steps and rail and a little moonlight pushed through the stone windows of the Lady Chapel, showing the portrait of the Byzantine virgin in her swirling circles of gold and blue, clutching her wide-eyed child.

I was about to leave when I saw him. He came out of the door leading from the vestry. At first I thought I was having a dream or a vision. He wore a cope. It seemed from where I was green, dark green with gold markings, and he walked very slowly and very quietly. Of course he had no shoes on, I remembered, and this slowness and silence gave him a strange and frightening dignity even though the cope was far too big and swept behind him, hissing across the parquet flooring as he moved up to the altar rails where he knelt and bowed his head; he knelt there a minute or two perhaps and then stood and opened the little wooden gate and moved up towards the altar itself. He stood in front of the tabernacle. I am sure his face was shining, except, of course, I never saw his face. Never again. I couldn't watch any more and getting very quietly to my feet I slipped from the church.

When Father Besserman insisted Vilakazi had gone

back to his own kind, I would have dearly liked to believe him. Instead I asked where I could find Brother Musel. Father Besserman, relieved of the responsibility, kept his arm around my shoulders and walked me into the vestry. We found it empty, cupboard doors ajar, smelling of beeswax, floor polish, disinfectant. Father Besserman chuckled. 'He's having a spring-cleaning. That's it. He is a shining man, Brother Musel. Scrupulous. You know what scrupulous means?'

'It's not spring, Father, it's nearly autumn.'

But there was no way past his implacable amiability. 'Yes. In Africa. But Brother Musel is a European at heart and in Europe now it's nearly spring. Go look for him in the boiler room. Maybe he never saw your friend, but it won't hurt to ask.'

The boiler room in the basement was large and brick-lined. Brother Musel was ironing a cassock on a big trestle table, the cloth flowing under the iron. The place was heavy with steam and the smell of soap and cinders. The clean surplices strung on a washing line across the room, stretched by their arms on the pegs, white, flaccid and somehow helpless, billowing gently in the currents of hot air from the furnace. The boiler hissed and ticked. Brother Musel went on ironing, his cassock sleeves rolled up above the elbow and the bunching muscles round as eggs gliding beneath the skin of his forearms. The furnace behind him kept up a slow steady roar and I could see through the observation window the coals banked up and gleaming fiercely, rich and ruddy like pirate's gold in picture books.

'Here is a cassock.' He handed me the cassock he'd been ironing, damply warm. 'Take a surplice from the line. Any one. All are clean. What I could not wash has gone to the dry cleaning. Everything is clean here now.'

He set the iron on its stand where it stood ticking, a smaller quicker sound than that the boiler gave off. Again that hum of his, a deep, tuneless, searching, as if he probed his own hidden depths. Then I noticed the picture. It was the photograph of a priest torn from a magazine. It lay beside the iron on the table.

'The boy is missing.'

'What boy is that?'

I grew restless, his studied indifference made me want to provoke him.

'I saw him on Saturday night.'

He shrugged, the humming deepened.

'It was in church, at the altar.'

'That cannot be. You are mistaken.'

'He was wearing a set of vestments and I think he carried a chalice.'

The terrible humming stopped. 'Are you mad? A native boy at the altar? I was in church on Saturday night. I was keeping vigil before the tabernacle. I saw nobody. You're making a joke with me, a bad, impious joke.'

'Where is Vilakazi, Brother Musel?'

'Why do you ask me?'

I pointed to the picture. 'That belonged to him.'

He picked up the picture. 'This I find in the pump-house. A pin had been driven through it. I suspect stray natives who plague the garden by night; stupid, ignorant people making witchcraft, voodoo. You know voodoo?'

'The boy lived in the pump-house.'

The large calm eyes regarded me. 'What boy?'

'The boy who owned the picture.'

He stared at me long and hard and then with a sudden movement he picked up the picture and deliberately crushed it. Screwing it up in his hand, holding his big, white-knuckled fist in the air between us and as if this was a ceremony, he crossed to the furnace, opened the door and threw the ball of paper inside where it flared on the golden coals, unclenched, and slowly died. Closing the door he turned his unsmiling face to me. 'What picture?'

I took my cassock and surplice smelling hot and clean, pressed it to my chest and went back to the sacristy. In the mirror I examined my face for signs of the knowledge I knew I carried within me. My face, as I'd half hoped, showed nothing of what it knew, though I could not make it meet my eyes. For an instant I almost persuaded myself that I owed it to that smooth, untroubled young face not to betray the innocence I saw there. It does not know, I said to myself, bending forward, and so you cannot know . . . then my nose touched the mirror and squinting upwards I saw, faintly darkening my forehead, the last few minute flakes of what had been my cross of ash.

Learning to Fly

Long ago, in the final days of the old regime, there lived a colonel who held an important job in the State Security Police and his name was Rocco du Preez. Colonel du Preez was in charge of the interrogation of political suspects and because of his effect on the prisoners of the old regime he became widely known in the country as 'Window jumpin'' du Preez. After mentioning his name it was customary to add 'thank God', because he was a strong man and in the dying days of the old regime everyone agreed that we needed a strong man. Now Colonel du Preez acquired his rather strange nickname not because he did any window jumping himself but rather because he had been the first to draw attention to this phenomenon which affected so many of the prisoners who were brought before him.

The offices of State Security were situated on the thirteenth floor of a handsome and tall modern block in the centre of town. Their high windows looked down on to a little dead-end street far below. Once this street had been choked with traffic and bustling with thriving shops. Then one day the first jumper landed on the roof of a car parked in the street and after that it was shut to traffic and turned into a pedestrian shopping mall. The street was filled in and covered over with crazy paving and one or two benches set up for weary shoppers. However, the jumpings increased. There were sometimes one or two a week and several nasty accidents on the ground began to frighten off the shoppers.

Whenever a jump had taken place the little street was cordoned off to allow in the emergency services: the police, the undertaker's men, the municipal workers brought in to hose down the area of impact which was often surprisingly large. The jumpings were bad for business and the shopkeepers grew desperate. The authorities were sympathetic and erected covered walk-ways running the length of the street leaving only the central area of crazy pavings and the benches, on which no one had ever been known to sit, exposed to the heavens: the walk-ways protected by their overhead concrete parapets were guaranteed safe against any and all flying objects. But still trade dwindled as one by one the shops closed, and the street slowly died and came to be known by the locals, who gave it a wide berth, as the 'landing field'.

As everyone knows, window jumpings increased apace over the years and being well placed to study them probably led Colonel Rocco du Preez to his celebrated thesis afterwards included in the manual of psychology used by recruits at the Police College and known as du Preez's Law. It states that all men, when brought to the brink, will contrive to find a way out if the least chance is afforded them and the choice of the means is always directly related to the racial characteristics of the individual in question. Some of du Preez's remarks on the subject have come down to us, though these are almost certainly apocryphal, as are so many tales of the final days of the old regime. 'Considering your average white man,' du Preez is supposed to have said, 'my experience is that he prefers hanging – whether by pyjama cord, belt, strips of blanket; providing he finds the handy protuberance, the cell bars, say, or up-ended bedstead, you'll barely have turned your back and he'll be up there swinging from the light cord or some other chosen noose. Your white man in his last throes has a wonderful sense of rhythm – believe me, whatever you may have heard to the contrary – I've seen several Whites about to cough it and all of them have been wonderful dancers. Your Indian, now, he's something else, a slippery customer who prefers smooth surfaces. I've known Asians to slip and crack their skulls in a shower cubicle so narrow you'd have sworn a man couldn't turn in it. This innate slitheriness is probably what makes them good businessmen. Now, your Coloured, per contra, is more clumsy a character altogether. His hidden talent lies in his amazing lack of co-ordination. Even the most sober rogue can appear hopelessly drunk to the untrained eye. On the surface of things it might seem that you can do nothing with him; he has no taste for the knotted strip of blanket or the convenient bootlace; a soapy bathroom floor leaves him unmoved – yet show him a short, steep flight of steps and he instinctively knows what to do. When it comes to Africans I have found that they, perverse as always, choose another way out. They are given to window jumping. This phenomenon has been very widespread in the past few years. Personally, I suspect its roots go back a long way, back to their superstitions – i.e. to their regard for black magic and witchcraft. Everyone knows that in extreme instances your average blackie will believe anything; that his witch-doctors will turn the white man's bullets to water; or, if he jumps out of a window thirteen storeys above terra firma he will miraculously find himself able to fly. Nothing will stop him once his mind's made up. I've seen up to six Bantu jump from a high window on one day. Though the first landed on his head and the others saw the result they were not deterred. It's as if despite the evidence of their senses they believed that if only they could practise enough they would one day manage to take off.'

'Window jumpin'' du Preez worked in an office sparsely furnished with an old desk, a chair, a strip of green, government-issue carpet, a very large steel cabinet marked 'Secret' and a bare, fluorescent light in the ceiling. Poor though the furnishings were, the room was made light and cheerful by the large windows behind his desk and nobody remembers being aware of the meanness of the furnishings when Colonel du Preez was present in the room. When he sat down in his leather swivel chair behind his desk, witnesses reported that he seemed to fill up the room, to make it habitable, even genial. His reddish hair and green eyes were somehow enough to colour the room and make it complete. The eyes had a peculiar, steady glint to them. This was his one peculiarity. When thinking hard about something he had the nervous habit of twirling a lock of the reddish hair, a copper colour with gingery lights, in the words of a witness, around a finger. It was his only nervous habit. Since these were often the last words ever spoken by very brave men, we have to wonder at their ability to register details so sharply under terrible conditions; it is these details that provide us with our only glimpse of the man, as no photographs have come down to us.

It was to this office that three plainclothes men one day brought a new prisoner. The charge-sheet was singularly bare: it read simply. 'Mpahlele . . . Jake. Possession of explosives'. Obviously they had got very little out of him. The men left closing the door softly, almost reverently, behind them.

The prisoner wore an old black coat, ragged grey flannels and a black beret tilted at an angle which gave him an odd, jaunty, rather continental look, made all the more incongruous by the fact that his hands were manacled behind him. Du Preez reached up with his desk ruler and knocked off the beret revealing a bald head gleaming in the overhead fluorescent light. It would have been shaved and polished, du Preez guessed, by one of the wandering barbers who traditionally gathered on Sundays down by the municipal lake, setting up three-legged stools and basins of water and hanging towels and leather strops for their cutthroat razors from the lower branches of a convenient tree and draping their customers in large red and white check cloths, giving them little hand mirrors so that they could look on while the barbers scraped, snipped, polished and gossiped away the sunny afternoon by the water's edge beneath the tall bluegums. Clearly Mpahlele belonged to the old school of whom there were fewer each year as the fashion for Afro-wigs and strange woollen bangs took increasing hold among younger Blacks. Du Preez couldn't help warming to this just a little. After all, he was one of the old school himself in the new age of trimmers and ameliorists. Mpahlele was tall, as tall as du Preez and, he reckoned, about the same age – though it was always difficult to tell with Africans. A knife scar ran from his right eye down to his collar, the flesh fused in a livid welt as if a tiny mole had burrowed under the black skin pushing up a furrow behind it. His nose had been broken, too, probably as the result of the same township fracas, and had mended badly turning to the left and then sharply to the right as if unable to make up its mind. The man was obviously a brawler. Mpahlele's dark brown eyes were remarkably calm – almost to the point of arrogance, du Preez thought for an instant, before dismissing the absurd notion with a tiny smile. It shocked him to see an answering smile on the prisoner's lips. However he was too old a hand to let this show.

'Where are the explosives?'

'I have no explosives,' Mpahlele answered.

He spoke quietly but du Preez thought he detected a most unjustifiable calm amounting to confidence, or worse, to insolence, and he noted how he talked with special care. It was another insight. On his pad he wrote the letters MK. The prisoner's diction and accent betrayed him. Mission Kaffir. Raised at one of the stations by foolish clergy as though he was one day going to be a white man. Of course, the word 'kaffir' was not a word in official use any longer. Like other names at that time growing less acceptable as descriptions of Africans: 'native', 'coon' and even 'Bantu', the word had given way to softer names in an attempt to respond to the disaffection springing up among black people. But du Preez, as he told himself, was too old a dog to learn new tricks. Besides, he was not interested in learning to be more 'responsive'. He did not belong to the ameliorists. His job was to control disaffection and where necessary to put it down with proper force. And anyway, his notes were strictly for his own reference, private reminders of his first impressions of a prisoner, useful when, and if, a second interview took place. The number of people he saw was growing daily and he could not expect to keep track of them all in his head.

Du Preez left his desk and slowly circled the prisoner. 'Your comrade who placed the bomb in the shopping centre was a bungler. There was great damage. Many people were killed. Women and children among them. But he wasn't quick enough, your friend. The blast caught him too. Before he died he gave us your name. The paraffin tests show you handled explosives recently. I want the location of the cache. I want the make-up of your cell with names and addresses as well as anything else you might want to tell me.'

'If the bomb did its business then the man was no bungler,' Mpahlele said.

'The murder of women and children – no bungle?'

Mpahlele shrugged. 'Casualties of war.'

Du Preez circled him and stopped beside his right ear. 'I don't call the death of children war. I call it barbarism.'

'Our children have been dying for years but we have never called it barbarism. Now we are learning. You and I know what we mean. I'm your prisoner of war. You will do whatever you can to get me to tell you things you want to know. Then you will get rid of me. But I will tell you nothing. So why don't you finish with me now? Save time.' His brown eyes rested briefly and calmly on du Preez's empty chair, and then swept the room as if the man had said all he had to say and was now more interested in getting to know that notorious office.

A muscle in du Preez's cheek rippled and it took him a moment longer than he would have liked to bring his face back to a decent composure. Then he crossed to the big steel cabinet and opened it. Inside was the terrible, tangled paraphernalia of persuasion, the electric generator, the leads and electrodes, the salt water for sharpening contact and the thick leather straps necessary for restraining the shocked and writhing victim. At the sight of this he scored a point; he thought he detected a momentary pause, a faltering in the steady brown eyes taking stock of his office, and he pressed home the advantage. 'It's very seldom that people fail to talk to me after this treatment.' He held up the electrodes. 'The pain is intense.'

In fact, as we know now, the apparatus in the cabinet was not that actually used on prisoners – indeed, one can see the same equipment on permanent exhibition in the National Museum of the Revolution. Du Preez, in fact, kept it for effect. The real thing was administered by a special team in a soundproof room on one of the lower floors. But the mere sight of the equipment, whose reputation was huge among the townships and shanty towns, was often enough to have the effect of loosening stubborn tongues. However, Mpahlele looked at the tangle of wires and straps as if he wanted to include them in his inventory of the room and his expression suggested not fear but rather – and this du Preez found positively alarming – a hint of approval. There was nothing more to be said. He went back to his desk, pressed the buzzer and the plainclothes men came in and took Mpahlele downstairs.

Over the next twenty-four hours 'Window jumpin'' du Preez puzzled over his new prisoner. It was a long time before he put his finger on some of the qualities distinguishing this man from others he'd worked with under similar circumstances. Clearly, Mpahlele was not frightened. But then other men had been brave too – for a while. It was not only bravery, one had to add to it the strange fact that this man quite clearly did not hate him. That was quite alarming: Mpahlele had treated him as if they were truly equals. There was an effrontery about this he found maddening and the more he thought about it, the more he raged inside. He walked over to the windows behind his desk and gazed down to the dead little square with its empty benches and its crazy paving which, with its haphazard joins where the stones were cemented one to the next into nonsensical, snaking patterns, looked from the height of the thirteenth storey as if a giant had brought his foot down hard and the earth had shivered into a thousand pieces. He was getting angry. Worse, he was letting his anger cloud his judgment. Worse still, he didn't care.

Mpahlele was in a bad way when they brought him back to du Preez. His face was so bruised that the old knife scar was barely visible, his lower lip was bleeding copiously and he swayed when the policemen let him go and might have fallen had he not grabbed the edge of the desk and hung there swaying. In answer to du Preez's silent question the interrogators shook their heads. 'Nothing. He never said *nothing*.'

Mpahlele had travelled far in the regions of pain and it had changed him greatly. It might have been another man who clung to du Preez's desk with his breath coming in rusty pants: his throat was choked with phlegm or blood he did not have the strength to cough away. He was bent and old and clearly on his last legs. One eye was puffed up in a great swelling shot with green and purple bruises, but the other, he noticed with a renewed spurt of anger, though it had trouble focusing, showed the same old haughty gleam when he spoke to the man.

'Have you any more to tell me about your war?'

Mpahlele gathered himself with a great effort, his one good eye flickering wildly with the strain. He licked the blood off his lips and wiped it from his chin. 'We will win,' he said, 'soon.'

Du Preez dismissed the interrogators with a sharp nod and they left his presence by backing away to the door, full of awe at his control. When the door closed behind them he stood up and regarded the swaying figure with its flickering eye. 'You are like children,' he said bitterly, 'and there is nothing we can do for you.'

'Yes,' said Mpahlele, 'we are your children. We owe you everything.'

Du Preez stared at him. But there was not a trace of irony to be detected. The madman was quite plainly sincere in what he said and du Preez found that insufferable. He moved to the windows and opened them. It was now that, so the stories go, he made his fateful remark. 'Well, if you won't talk, then I suppose you had better learn to fly.'

What happened next is not clear except in broad outline even today, the records of the old regime which were to have been made public have unaccountably been reclassified as secret, but we can make an informed guess. Legend then says that du Preez recounted for his prisoner his 'theory of desperate solutions' and that, exhausted though he was, Mpahlele showed quickening interest in the way out chosen by white men – that is to say, dancing. We know this is true because du Preez told the policemen waiting outside the door when he joined them in order to allow Mpahlele to do what he had to do. After waiting a full minute, du Preez entered his office again closing the door behind him, alone, as had become customary in such cases, his colleagues respecting his need for a few moments of privacy before moving on to the next case. Seconds later these colleagues heard a most terrible cry. When they rushed into the room they found it was empty.

Now we are out on a limb. We have no more facts to go on. All is buried in obscurity or say, rather, it is buried with du Preez who plunged from his window down to the landing field at the most horrible speed, landing on his head. Jake Mpahlele has never spoken of his escape from Colonel 'Window jumpin'' du Preez. All we have are the stories. Some firmly believe to this day that it was done by a special magic and Mpahlele had actually learnt to fly and that the colonel on looking out of his window was so jealous at seeing a black man swooping in the heavens that he had plunged after him on the supposition, regarded as axiomatic in the days of the old regime, that anything a black man could do, a white man could do ten times better. Others, more sceptical, said that the prisoner had hidden himself in the steel cabinet with the torture equipment and emerged to push du Preez to hell and then escaped in the confusion you will get in a hive if you kill the queen bee. All that is known for sure is that du Preez lay on the landing field like wet clothes fallen from a washing line, terribly twisted and leaking everywhere. And that in the early days of the new regime Jake Mpahlele was appointed chief investigating officer in charge of the interrogation of suspects and that his work with political prisoners, especially white prisoners, was soon so widely respected that he won rapid promotion to the rank of colonel and became known throughout the country as Colonel Jake 'Dancin'' Mpahlele, and after his name it was customary to add 'thank God', because he was a strong man and in the early days of the new regime everyone agreed we needed a strong man.

My Stigmata

I remember the morning I found that I had the wounds. I got up and went downstairs to the bathroom, holding my side, the pain was that bad. On my way I met my landlady, Doris Clench. 'I think I've got the stigmata, Mrs Clench,' I said.

'Garn,' she said.

'No, really.' Nodding vigorously, I pushed past her to the bathroom, the better to examine the extent of the damage.

My left side was pierced by a red raw wound about the size of a shilling. My hands and feet carried the traditional marks. They looked like bullet holes, dead centre through each palm and neat, with no ragged edges, covered by a transparent membrane through which the red flesh gleamed. Anxiously I explored my hairline in the mirror for signs of the crown of thorns, but it seemed that I was spared that at least. On second thoughts, it didn't cheer me up much because I remembered that exterior stigmatization may be preceded by invisible stigmata, as happened with the celebrated Padre Pio. But then Pio had been a natural candidate for the honour, and honour it is among mystics. What with his levitation during the consecration of the mass and his almost supernatural percipience in the confessional, you could have said that he was asking for it. But not me. It was only because I was a lapsed Catholic that I had recognized the symptoms, but for the rest I was barely a Christian, and I certainly wasn't religious. Something was very wrong, somewhere.

As I made my careful way up the stairs to my room, I met my neighbour, Mr Patel. We did not get on too well. He had a succession of icy blondes coming to his room most nights and the bumps and groans and shrieks in the small hours kept me awake. I hadn't had a decent night's sleep in weeks. Mr Patel made the point of apologizing to me on every possible occasion for the exuberance of his lovers. They became too excited, he explained. I did not want to speak to him, but one look at his face showed me that there was no escaping. His smooth hand rested on my sleeve. 'Courage, my friend.'

'I suppose Mrs Clench told you?'

He nodded and patted me on the shoulder gingerly. He kept glancing at my hands which were sunk in the pockets of my dressing gown.

'It is a holy affliction.'

'It's a bloody tragedy.' As I fumbled at the door of my room with my key, I noticed that he had not moved and was gazing up the stairwell at me, his eyes liquid with concern.

'The love of God can hurt a man,' he called.

I managed to get my door open. 'Yes,' I said, 'especially when he gets too excited.'

I went into my room and sat on my bed for what must have been at least an hour, maybe more. It was some while later, anyway, that I snapped out of it. There was no point sitting there like a dummy. I had to get out and about. I put on gloves and carpet slippers and went downstairs.

Outside the sun was shining and the sky was a blank and lovely blue. The sun lit up the vacant little park across the way, the 'gardens' from which the neighbourhood took its name, with its locked gates to which only the oldest in the Victorian boarding houses flanking the road had keys and there were fewer of those each year.

Obviously there was no question of my going to work,

wearing gloves and carpet slippers, my body a dull ache. I could not go back to my desk at the Imperial Insurance Company and continue writing all risks policies covering the jewels of rich women. I could not give up my mind to anything at that moment but to the control of the pain that bent me double, dogged my footsteps and held my hands tightly.

There was nothing for it but to see the doctor. I sat in the waiting room, leaning up against the frosted glass, reading an article in *Life* about outer space and the universe and how if one imagined the sun as an orange then the earth was no bigger than a pea, or something, a hundred miles away. At last the light went on above one of the brown-painted doors and the nurse called my name and showed me in to the doctor.

He was very kind. I removed my left glove and he made a thorough examination of the wound. 'A nasty business,' he said.

'I have another on my right hand,' I told him.

'Gracious me!' he snorted, 'you've really been in the wars, haven't you? We'd better have your shirt off.'

'Actually, I have two identical holes in my feet,' I said, as casually as I could, struggling with my shirt buttons. I took off all my clothes then and lay down on the bed.

He drew in his breath sharply when he saw me. 'Who has injured you like this?' he demanded.

'I think it was an accident,' I said.

'Well,' he said, after examining me closely, 'the least I can do is to dress them. Though, I'll hand it to you, you've kept them remarkably clean without the use of bandages and antiseptic. How you managed it, I don't know. Anyway, I'll give you something for them and then, remember please, a clean dressing every morning.' He bent to examine the wounds again. They fascinated him, I could see that. Clearly, he didn't want me to put on my clothes yet. 'Remarkable symmetry about them,' he said. 'Of course, if you had come to me earlier, I'd have stitched them for you. It's too late now. They're healing.'

I walked home. Mrs Clench and her three daughters awaited me in the hallway. Mrs Clench's daughters attended a convent school. All looked at me with earnest eyes.

'So we're off to work, are we?' Mrs Clench asked, not unkindly.

Her daughters eyed me hopefully. What did they expect me to do? I smiled as best I could and went upstairs to my room. The pain was no worse. No better, but no worse. The dressings the doctor had used were comfortable and maybe he was right about the wounds healing. Voices were raised in the hallway below. I lay down on my bed and closed my eyes. Clearly, the news was getting around.

In the morning I dressed the wounds. I could detect no change in their glassy surface although they seemed to throb less painfully. I put on my gloves and carpet slippers and went down for a walk. A small crowd had gathered outside the door. Mrs Clench was addressing interested neighbours. They stopped talking when they saw me and looked embarrassed. Two mild men in grey raincoats pressed forward.

'Hansome, of *The Times*,' said the taller of the two, holding out his hand.

'How do you do.' I kept my hands firmly in my pockets.

'My photographer, Pounder, Rutland Pounder.' His companion nodded cheerily. 'I wonder if you would mind if we spoke to you briefly about the rather strange situation in which you find yourself?'

The neighbours smiled encouragingly. They knew, their smiles assured me, that perhaps this wasn't a proper occasion for the press, but it was after all *The Times*.

'Come inside,' I said, 'we can talk in my room.'

The pictures the next morning were very good and the story beside them was concise and lucid, not at all sensational. I found myself reading it with interest. Although now a stigmatic, I was very far from being an expert on the subject. I wondered if the doctor who had treated me took *The Times*.

As I neared home with the newspaper I saw the neighbours gathered in what was now a regular knot on the steps before Mrs Clench's front door. I saw, too, a bus parked by the kerb, a school bus. Ranged next to it was a long, orderly crocodile of convent girls. I recognized the uniform as being the same as that worn by the young Clench girls. I stopped dead and then, of course, just as I realized I should get away quickly, they saw me. A fat, brisk nun with silver hair and rosy cheeks trotted up to me and bobbed a knee. She and her girls were there, she explained frankly, in the hopes of meeting me. The young Clench girls had talked at school about their mother's lodger who had been blessed with Christ's five glorious wounds. Nobody had paid very much attention to them until the report appeared in *The Times*. She and her girls had not come to stare, but to look and to marvel at the works of God.

'It's a very wonder the marks the good Jesus puts upon the man.' Her Irish lisp conveyed her sentiment and I was reminded of my schooldays, when it was always an Irish voice that led the general prayers in the parish church after confessions each Friday. Mind you, it was a Jewish boy who'd led the prayers in the classroom when the bell rang on the hour and the class rose to recite the Hail Mary as they did again at twelve o'clock for the Angelus. From then on all prayers for me were prayed in Irish or Jewish voices and even the tones of those voices in banal conversation took on a sacral quality recalling the giant Christ who swung in agony upon his cross above the high altar in the cool gloom of the parish church when we prayed our communal prayers on those Friday mornings after confession. Outside one could hear the doves calling in the fir trees. It was very peaceful and miles from school and almost worth praying for. Often I was tempted to sneak out of the side door as we left the church to straggle back to the classroom and to hide myself behind the hedge that flanked the garden and orchards and sit there in the sun. Just sit there, quietly, untouched by anything but my own thoughts as the sun moved higher in the sky, warming my bones.

'I'm sorry,' I said, looking into her blue eyes, 'but what can I say? I have all the wounds, but this is not the place . . .'

'Except the crown,' she said.

'Except the crown,' I agreed. 'I've been spared that.'

'It takes some differently, my dear,' she said. 'Now, Maria Razzi of Chio, why, she had the thorny crown alone.'

'You've made a study of it, Sister?'

She beamed. 'We're doing a project in class.'

She took her girls away, with some giggling and downcast looks in the rear files of the crocodile. She seemed moved. I walked inside without a glance at the little groups of people who stood on either side of the street before the rows of silent houses, talking and staring.

That tour of the convent girls and their sweet-cheeked teacher was the start of a wave of publicity that hit that afternoon and continued for a week. In that time I was assailed by people wherever I went, wanting to know how I felt, the extent of my pain, the shape of my wounds, the health of my soul, the heat of my faith, my plans for the future. Worst were those who made joking allusions to Doubting Thomas and licked their lips, not daring to ask me out loud to let them see and touch my stigmata.

The day after the visit of the convent girls, a great scarlet coachload of bishops drew up outside Mrs Clench's house, and a deputation of their lordships entered to greet me. They had come, I was assured, not to gape, but to congratulate me. They had learnt that I was an unwilling stigmatic and so they hoped that I would not take it amiss and feel even more put upon were they to offer me their warmest greetings and prayerful good wishes. They were immensely grateful for this wonder that had been worked in me, and however vicarious their satisfaction might appear to me to be, I was respectfully asked to bear with them in their joy at the greatest fillip Christianity had received in England for decades. Stigmata had become more common in comparatively recent times, perhaps through devotion to the Sacred Heart, but that was hardly an English practice. Indeed my stigmata seemed to fill the bishops with much the same confidence and enthusiasm as my role at the Imperial Insurance Company did for rich women by making certain that their jewels, even if by some horrid catastrophe reduced to their natural elements, would retain their value in our books at least.

I saw the bishops off, talking happily, all smiles and waves, and turned inside. I was moving a little more easily. The pain was still there. But it was no worse. It seemed hard now to imagine a time when I had not had this dull ache in hands, feet and side. Perhaps I was getting used to it.

Mr Patel stood in the entrance hall holding the public telephone which served us all in the house.

'It's the *Psychic News* on the line,' he whispered, covering the mouthpiece. 'They want to talk to you.'

I looked at him. I could think of nothing to say.

'I shall tell them that you are indisposed.'

I went upstairs to bed. I washed my wounds and applied the antiseptic and dressings the doctor had given me but I did so more out of habit than conviction. The wounds seemed unaffected by the treatment. They seemed to have a being of their own, affixed to myself, but independent of me. Then I settled into a long, dreamless sleep.

In the morning I awoke almost refreshed and reflected that, perhaps, my strangeness was being made too much of, by myself as well as by others. Men had fragile, paper-thin skins, which wrinkled and tore easily. My tears were coincidentally localized, that was all. Altogether, I decided, there was too much fuss being made. My stigmata had become too much of a good thing.

It was early yet and the house was asleep. I decided to take a walk, donned my carpet slippers and gloves, and went quietly downstairs. But I had no sooner opened the door and taken a breath of the morning freshness when windows and doors opened all around me. There were faces at panes. Dogs barked, the milkman arrived and housewives appeared on the doorsteps with their dogs and children and husbands and gazed at me. I lost my nerve and closed the door. Perhaps I would venture out later.

Mrs Clench faced me in the dark hallway. She smiled encouragingly. In her hands she held a copy of *The Times*. I took it. She had opened it at the centre page which carried the editorials. Her eyes were shining. I followed her trembling finger and understood the cause of her excitement. I was the subject of the third editorial.

What can be said of this young man? He has been visited by a strange and novel experience. One which is perhaps even more shocking since it comes to him without either his knowledge or his encouragement. His behaviour in this matter has been exemplary. So much more so than that of those people who have taken an interest in his religious experience. We salute him. It might be thought by some in these Islands that the phenomenon which he has experienced is confined to those who embrace the Church of Rome. This extraordinary, some will say miraculous, event, has given proof, if proof were needed, that the division of faith is the failure of our times – and nonsense, to boot. Besides, there is no room, surely, as recent and bloody events not far removed from us have shown, for this sort of sectarian prejudice.

'Well . . . yes,' I thought.

Sometime later I slipped outside by the back door. I could not stand being cooped up any longer. I put on my gloves and slippers and, after a moment's thought, a black woollen balaclava helmet. No one recognized me as I walked swiftly through the morning sunshine. I came to a pond, spanned by a narrow little bridge, where people stopped and gathered to talk.

'They say that he has holes, gaping holes, nail marks in his hands and feet, Doris says, though she's never seen them,' a little old lady, well wrapped in green coat and muffler, was saying to another in a red trench coat and wellingtons.

'Ever so painful they must be, too,' the other agreed. 'I saw the pictures in *The Times*. And him not even the least bit religious.'

'I know,' said the little lady, 'it's not nice, is it?'

'Of course you can't believe everything you read in the papers, now can you? I mean, Doris didn't actually *see* these wounds, did she? I mean, she saw the photos in *The Times*, same as we did. That's all. And she says that he doesn't go to work any longer.'

'You've got a point there,' her friend nodded.

'And you know, sometimes I think these people bring

these things on themselves. Besides, we all have our problems, don't we?'

But she had lost the attention of her companion who had turned and was looking straight at me.

'Didn't you say that he dressed in gloves and carpet slippers?'

'So Doris said.'

Then they were both looking at me. I put my head down and walked away entering my boarding house by the back door. I had hoped to avoid meeting anybody. But once again Mrs Clench accosted me at the foot of the stairs. I eyed her defiantly through my balaclava helmet. In the silence I became aware of my heavy breathing.

She eyed me with faint curiosity. 'No change?'

I shook my head and went up to my room, undressed and got into bed. By seven o'clock that evening, I was still awake. Several bumps, a groan and a giggle behind the wall told me that Mr Patel's lovers were once again becoming too excited.

Hilton Hits Back

In the matter of orphans, politics is a cruel stepmother. I blame myself entirely for this discovery since it was I who made the family connection in the first place, and for no good reason either. None at all. I've always been one of those rather singular orphans who enjoyed being without parents. I revelled in the so-called disadvantage and, while this made me the odd man out during my time at St Joseph's Home for Boys, up on the Ridge, it paid off when I left St Joe's and went on to university where I found everyone working like crazy to blot out all family connections and transform themselves into orphans. After years of enduring the agony of having the gaps in my life forcibly plugged with tatty foster parents and spurious 'aunts', the campus was a liberation and a home-coming. That's why, when I was asked by Hilton van Fölter what I thought of it all, I told him it was a picnic.

Hilton's girl of the month, Sharon, scoffed at Hilton's interest in me. I was, she said, 'a political naif'. And when I looked it up, I decided she was right. When she asked me point blank if I was aware that 'Africans were being crucified on the altar of apartheid'? I had to confess I did not. In fact, I knew nothing at all about Africans. At St Joseph's they were simply the people who polished the floors and got drunk and stabbed each other during wild parties in the servant's quarters on Saturday nights and their screams in the night were merely a component of the African soundscape, blending with the shrilling crickets and the frogs. Of course, in my first six weeks on campus, before I met Hilton, I began to get a political education: I became dimly aware that apartheid was bad; it made black people suffer and it was up to us to oppose it. You could say I was developing the usual, vague, liberal leanings. I'd never been on a protest march and never attended a mass student meeting. But then commerce students didn't much go in for that sort of thing. I got the impression that it was more the province of the 'arts' crowd who were led by the hard men in the student radical movement, and the hard men were led by Hilton van Fölter. All this changed when Hilton recruited me for what he called my great advantage, my 'radical orphanhood'.

Hilton was the old man of the campus and the champion fighter for racial equality. No one knew *how* old he was, though I've heard his age put at twenty-seven. Personally, I feel that's rather exaggerated. No one knew what course he was taking and if you asked them, people in the know muttered something vague about 'honours', in politics perhaps. Others said it was social anthropology. He went to no lectures though he could be seen everywhere on the campus, a bulky, untidy figure in a cracked panama, flapping along in old grey flannels and torn sandals over the edges of which his black, uncut toenails protruded like the eaves of a roof. I'd never met anyone who cared so little about how he looked. Fresh out of the orphanage as I was, where darning, patching and polishing, turning shirt collars and dropping hems did more than keep clothes on the back, they stitched the world together, and proud of my first team school tie and blue barathea blazer, a present from the Rector, overcome that a boy from 'the Home' should have won a full scholarship to university, I looked on Hilton's extravagant sloppiness as an illness, a destructive disease, the deliberate murder of the duty to turn out looking clean and neat in public, drummed into us at St Joseph's as being the poor child's only defence in a sharp-eyed, mercenary world.

When Hilton one day collared me on the campus and talked politics, furiously fanning himself with his panama in the sweltering heat, the mechanical summer sunshine that seemed to switch itself on every morning and rose to an unvarying solar whine, shrillest at noon and burning through the afternoon in skies like white ash, I found myself turning my face away when he spoke in case I picked up a trace of his disease. I overcame this prejudice during the mammoth seminar on Marxist politics he gave me over the next weeks and was soon breathing in the air he breathed out as if I'd been doing it all my life though I never could turn out on campus looking anything but clean and neat. As it happened, I was to pay dearly for this.

'This may look like a picnic to you, tootling around the place in collar and tie like a Jehovah's Witness on house calls, but I invite you to look again. What you are seeing is a battlefield.'

Obediently, I peered about me at the bright, noisy campus crowded with sports cars and motor bikes: I saw girls in bikinis shining like buttered kippers under their suntan oil, who lay soaking up the sun around the ornamental fountains; I watched as others in tiny shorts or shocking pink ski-pants strolled between lectures arm in arm with white-coated medics or stocky engineers in baggy khaki shorts and traditional thick woollen socks. I saw a scratch team from my commerce class score against a team of grey-suited lawyers in a game of touch rugby beside the swimming pool. I said I thought much of the fighting must be going on beneath the surface.

'It's a war to the death,' Hilton assured me. 'We are out to smash the system. This means hitting our parents.

That's tough. But the old wrinklies are usually the system's first line of defence.'

I noticed how many girls waved at Hilton who flapped his panama in return with a careless flourish. His reputation as an 'older' man and a political wildman was a potent attraction. They said he was so popular that he took his women on a strict rota and limited himself to one a month.

'I'm an orphan.'

'Really? I had to fight for my freedom. You're one up on me there. Tragedy aside, it's a headstart. Stay lucky like that always.'

Hilton's own struggle against his parents was campus legend and every freshman heard it about two minutes after arriving. Hilton's family were rich. His father was a pure capitalist who ran an airline and sent his son up to university to become a dentist. One afternoon, in the middle of a lab practical on elementary exodontics, he collapsed at his bench. Some said he faked it but Hilton swore he had had a vision of a new society based on racial justice and equity, 'probably on a par with St Paul's, if not higher,' was how his girl of the month, Sharon, explained it to me. Anyway the upshot of it was that he disowned his father, gave up his silk shirts, his Dunhill pipe and his cut-price holiday flights to places like Bermuda, dropped out of dentistry and enrolled in the course on 'Politics and Existence' given by the legendary neo-Hegelian, B. F. E. Lestrade, 'Buffy' to his friends and adoring students, until the sad business of the Registrar's nephew gave his enemies their chance to hound him from his job and the country, a ruined man, though retaining to the last enough of his stinging humour to tell a brash reporter who asked sneeringly about his plans at a press conference organized by Hilton and a few staunch admirers that he was off to Hamburg where he planned to open a male brothel. At the time of his vision, when he booted dentures into touch, Hilton's reading didn't extend beyond, say, Black's *Operative Dentistry*. Buffy Lestrade introduced him to Marx and the rest is history.

'Buffy's father, believe it or not,' Hilton told me with a grin during my new political education, 'was actually a semiprofessional soccer player. Can you credit it? He played on the right wing for Callies. Imagine the leap Buffy had to make to get out of that hole! It led him to develop his theory about the vital need to maintain the split between child and parent as the way to kill off old, engrained racial thinking in this country. Of course, most kids at university go through the rejection stage; a year killing off parents, a year adjusting to freedom, a year of political struggle and then, sadly, the inevitable degree, a job in a mining house and return to the family fold. Buffy saw that we had to really work at widening the generation gap. 'Radical orphanhood' – to speak in Lestradian terms – now that's what we're after in the progressive movement. And that's where you score. You're a natural.'

In our two-week, walking seminar Hilton told me about the economic basis of racialism, the institutionalizing of alienation, the one-dimensional, or what he called the 'flat-map' distortion of African history, and the dialectics of protest. It was, he confessed modestly, no more than theoretical structure. Even the protest marches and demonstrations were theoretical. This was the stage the struggle had reached. He looked towards the day when we'd move beyond the battle of words and begin to act, to seize the chance of genuinely authentic existence, to make something *real* happen.

Stencilled on the side of the old rucksack Hilton used as a book bag was a row of policeman's helmets, set out like fighter-pilots chalk up their 'kills'. Each helmet stood for an arrest. The number of his arrests – some twelve to date – on demonstration marches was the toast of the illicit late-night parties held in safe houses in the suburbs where radical black and white students met, mingled, drank and danced together. I never got to any of those. Well, I did go once, on the night before my first protest march, with a rather plain girl called Dodie from my elementary statistics class who shared my liberal yearnings and had a car to boot. But we couldn't find parking. At least, not until it was too late, because the place was solid with limousines for blocks around. We finally made it as the party was packing up. Nobody told me you were supposed to get there late for safety's sake, but not too late or otherwise the student cars jammed the streets for blocks around and the security police who always followed them and invariably gate-crashed the party pretending to be drunken accountants, or radical theology students, would grab what little parking remained.

'The really old hands form lift-clubs,' Sharon revealed pityingly when I told her about it. She was in second-year sociology, blonde, terribly tense, so painfully thin that the bony hollows on each side of her neck looked as if they would have held half a cup of water apiece. She had this habit of turning her head away while she was speaking and looking at you out of the corner of her eye. She was the sort of girl who carried her conscience in a holster. 'And what's your field?' Her glance took in my barathea blazer and tie.

'First-year commerce. I've never been on a march before. Shall I nip back to my rooms and change?'

She gave me a look of remorseless sympathy. 'We all have our cross. No, don't change. It's strictly come as you are.'

We had assembled to pick up our banners and posters

for the march on the central police station in town. All the protest material had been made by the girls of the Student Christian Association under Sharon's direction. There was a fine selection of placards many with hand-embroidered slogans, others stiff with red ribbon rosettes; some were even done in batik and others stamped with original African wood-cuts. Hilton went to a lot of trouble choosing something suitable for me.

'As this is your first time, I think you ought to be allowed to make a bit of a show. What about this one? The reference is especially apt. I like my material to have point and communicate fast. Can't mince words. Most of the crowd who see our marches are as thick as two planks. You will march up front and tell the so-called electorate exactly what we think of the people they've voted into power and I hope it jolly well stings.'

That's how I came to lead the march of several hundred students carrying a placard bearing a big, grainy blown-up photograph of the prime minister over the challenging question: *A Vote for Barabbas*? The police were to take strong exception to this and, truth be told, I had to agree with them. Personally, I've always considered our prime minister looked more like a sinister medieval pontiff. I suppose it's the veiny nose and the sunken eyes that give the impression, and of course, the little shining cap of hair combed flat strengthens the papal look. The eyes are sunken and of so light a blue they seem almost colourless, like drying water-holes, receding into their sockets leaving the surrounding banks of flesh seamed and folded like river sand. All in all, a profligate pope more likely to be given to highly individual vices behind consistory doors than petty thievery. But there you are – Hilton van Fölter said it must be Barabbas and Barabbas it was.

I offered to take off my tie.

'Do you feel too dressed?' Hilton asked. '*Per contra*. We want that, I think. It's the shocking difference, you see, between the look of you, as it were, stiff and formal and clean, and the poster you're carrying.' For some reason he was wearing an old leather flying helmet and enormous gauntlets. 'Who would imagine such a conventional guy – ' he smashed a fist into his palm – 'could pack such a punch!'

Sharon looked sceptical. 'Don't you think, Hilt, that pushing him out front, especially with *that* placard, is risky? It makes him look so, well, prominent. The cops could just possibly home in on him. And this is his first time. A baby accountant in his blazer and tie.'

'But that's just it! There is something symbolic about it, something vestal, even. Picture it. The virgin out front, pure and undefiled. Yet he carries – and here we score, he's carrying this profane message challenging, attacking the onlookers. Do you realize that were it not for their uniforms the cops would be onlookers too? Don't forget they're also human, just as open to the force of symbols, just as liable to be taken by our street theatre. Who knows, one day we might score with them. As for handling himself, remember I've taught this boy all I know.'

'And he couldn't have had a better teacher – but it's still all theory.'

Hilton bridled. 'For God's sake, Shar – theory! This fellow's a professional orphan. He knows more about holding out against the old guard than you and I put together.' He turned on me. 'Right?'

Of course, I had no option then. The honour of orphans was at stake. 'Right.'

'Besides,' Hilton gave his famous hurt, modest half-smile, and touched her cheek soothingly, 'remember we're up there with him. If they do jump, I think we all know who they're likely to land on.'

Sharon melted. She lifted a flap of helmet and kissed his ear. 'Okay Hilt. I believe.'

Hilton briefed us then, cupping his gloved hands so his voice boomed. 'I won't say much. Most of you know the ropes but for the benefit of newcomers I'll just go over salient points. Once we reach the police station sit down. Placards must be legible at all times. I'll make a short speech. The cops will then read the riot act and order us to disperse. Please, this is very important, *please* don't move until I give the signal. Perfect timing is crucial. It's important that we leave after the warning but *before* they charge and judging that is a delicate matter. Keep your eyes on me. When we withdraw, do so in a body, with placards – and I can't repeat this too often – placards held high, banners taut. Thank you.'

I hadn't imagined the police might turn nasty. It gave me a slight tremor.

'But what happens if they pick on us?'

'Sit tight,' Sharon advised. 'A good rule of thumb is – if in doubt, don't hit back. It only makes matters worse.'

'Just keep your eyes on me,' Hilton repeated, sadly, wearily, his face moonishly grave in the circle of the flying helmet. 'And if you see them land on me, don't panic. You're not here to save me. You're expressing solidarity with the oppressed and don't forget it. Besides, I'm more or less prepared for anything they may throw at me. Comes of practice.'

'Practice makes perfect,' Sharon said quietly. I laughed.

'It's not a joke.' She was cross. 'Hilton has borne the worst of the police attacks. He's been hurt so often, I sometimes think he is trying to perfect his life through suffering. Like a saint.'

We marched in threes. I was placed between Hilton and Sharon and we led the waving column out of the university grounds under the great arch, surmounted by a bronze giantess with her arm thrown around the neck of a young doe signifying 'Hope in Pursuit of Peace', past the fountain opposite the main gates where a granite lioness, symbolizing Mother Africa, suckled four identical cubs representing the four major racial groups each with its sacred right to separate but equal freedoms, and into the heavy traffic moving towards town. The importance of my position gave me butterflies and I wished I'd eaten before leaving. I noticed that several students had brought along packed lunches. Old hands.

We snaked along the side of the road in a fairly disciplined column, which was something of an achievement because we came in for a lot of stick from passing motorists who seemed to delight in driving dangerously close, hooting, pulling monkey faces and jeering at us. The beefy driver of a blue Zephyr slowed down to a snail's pace and rolled down his window. Hilton ignored him. Leaning on a freckled, meaty muscled arm stuck on the door-jamb, he advised us to get our hair cut.

'Fascist,' Hilton retorted, not missing a step.

'Bloody commie.'

'Rockspider.'

The beefy man acknowledged this traditional insult by switching into his native Afrikaans with a terrible oath about Hilton's mother's womb.

'My mother is Africa,' Hilton replied, also in Afrikaans.

'Looking at you – she's been sleeping around.' And he roared away.

'Thanks for the compliment!' Hilton shrieked after him. The straps of his flying helmet danced about his ears and we all cheered wildly and it felt more like a picnic than ever.

The central police station was a tall skyscraper that could be mistaken for one of the banks or insurance companies which surrounded it. We sat down on the pavement and Hilton made a speech calling for an end to racism and segregated buses; I seem to remember he demanded also that the municipality make liquor licences available to student canteens and ended by quoting Abe Lincoln who had once said that for evil to succeed it was enough that good men remained silent. A burst of rowdy applause greeted this compliment which Hilton acknowledged with a confident thumbs-up. I'm afraid that I got rather carried away at this point and jumped up calling for three cheers for Hilton. Sharon shushed me.

The police faced us with water-hoses. The station commander, red-faced, irritable, speaking through a megaphone, warned us that the demonstration was illegal. Hilton responded with the flurry of sign language indicating that we should sit down in the road and keep quiet. When we had settled down the commander, after much smoothing of his grey drooping moustache, read us the riot act, or rather he quoted it from memory in a stilted way, like an actor with a hazy grasp of his lines. I noticed how carefully everything was staged, it was a sort of play in which everyone knew their parts. If we did not leave quietly, the commander warned, we would be dispersed with all necessary force. Again, Hilton's eloquent gestures told us to sit tight. The police held a huddled conference and a large constable came deliberately down the steps to where we sat stiff and proud at the head of our brave demonstration. I felt Hilton tense beside me. He foresaw another helmet on his book bag. Instead, blow me down, if the cop didn't grab me and demand that I go with him. When I refused he grabbed me under the elbows and began heaving me up the steps. Hilton jumped up furious and tried to stop him. This clearly wasn't in the script. Sharon shrieked that they had no right to arrest me. Hilton said that this was my first time. Sharon explained that I was 'only a commerce student'. The constable put me down, drew his truncheon and hit Hilton hard and low in the groin, I think, because he dropped like a stone. Sharon screamed that they had murdered him. Then the cops with the hoses turned them on full force, working with a terrible nonchalance; they might have been hosing down their driveways on a hot Sunday afternoon and in about two minutes flat they'd cleared the road.

Once they got me inside the police seemed to lose interest. Certainly, I wasn't much of a catch. It had been the poster they were after. Sharon had been right. After examining it mournfully, the commander pointed out its inaccuracy. If I'd compared the prime minister with, say, Genghis Khan, or Hitler, that would have been typical student abuse. But to compare him with a common thief, and with this particular thief, was beyond the pale. The desk sergeant, a young man called Hattingh, said blasphemy made him want to vomit. He demanded my first-team tie as well as my watch and spare cash, on the grounds that a prisoner had recently hung himself with his long-johns and he didn't want me getting ideas. But I noticed he spoke without much hope.

The constable who arrested me took me down to the cells in the basement. The feeling seemed to be that since he'd pulled me in, I was his problem. His name was Swanepoel, Swannie to his colleagues. The lock-ups weren't too bad, if rather dirty, painted in government green with double bunks, a slop pail and one small window high up and heavily barred, the thick, greenish glass bleary with dust.

'What gives you people the right to trample all over people's religious beliefs?' Swanepoel demanded.

I saw my chance and spoke to him at some length, and rather well too, if I may say so myself, about the economic basis of racialism. He heard me out in silence and when I finished he spat carefully into a corner of my cell and said that I hadn't answered his question.

But I wasn't giving in that easily. 'What gives you the right to trample all over black people?'

He lifted one boot then the other with studied concentration. 'Black people,' he called softly, 'come out little black people, Old Swannie's not going to hurt you.'

Two could play that game. I sat on my bunk and took a foot in my hand and examined the sole of my boot minutely while he looked on, puzzled. 'Not a trampled principle in sight,' I shook my head sadly. 'Not a trace.'

He took off his cap and squinted at me suspiciously. Then he laughed. Seeing him there twisting his cap in his big hands until the grommet popped, with his toothy grin and close-cropped, blond hair, it came as a shock to realize that he couldn't have been much older than me.

'You've got me there, Barabbas. That's the trouble with playing with words. I'm tired of words. I want action. It's time something happened. Something real.'

'What do you mean *real*? What's more real than *apartheid*?'

He put on his cap and shrugged. 'Trouble with you guys is that you're so damn superior.'

That really stung. 'Listen, I'm not superior. I'm in jail for not being superior and for wanting to smash the system.'

He grinned again. 'Cheap talk. It's no great shakes to be in jail, you know. You're too stuck up to see you couldn't smash your way out of a paper bag.'

'And who am I supposed to be superior to?'

He winked. 'Folks like me,' he said, and he was gone.

An investigation of my cell brought a joyful discovery. If I climbed on to the top bunk I could reach the window bars and haul myself up to the grimy pane and get a blurred ankle-level view of the street directly outside the station. I could hold myself up only for a few minutes at a time but it was enough. It was from this vantage point that I watched the second demonstration later that day.

A column of students, mostly the same lot who had marched that morning, carrying new banners and placards, led the way and formed up on the pavement across the road from the police station. Here was a heavy iron gate barring the entrance to an alley which ran between two buildings. A naked man bent double under a cross made of some blond wood staggered up to the iron gate. It was Hilton, of course. A working party lowered the cross to the ground and when they raised it up again he was fixed to it and the cross was bound to the gate with ropes, or perhaps chains. Hilton was not naked as I'd thought but he wore a pair of tiny black and yellow, fake-leopard skin underpants. A woman in flowing black, and heavily veiled, pushed her way through the crowd and took up a position at the foot of the cross and I knew this silent, shrouded mourner was she of the bird-bath shoulders, Hilton's girl of the month, Sharon. I also knew that Hilton was going for broke. My arrest must have been the last straw. In the face of his advice to me, Hilton had decided to hit back.

There were police everywhere, charging furiously with batons drawn. It was like watching a silent film. For a few minutes the air flocked with torn posters and flying caps and bristled with sticks as the cops laid about them. Some removed their heavy leather belts and whipped the demonstrators. The dogs followed, huge Alsatians bounding ahead of their handlers, straining at their short leads and making snarling rushes at the few students left on their feet. One of the dogs leaped at the sorrowing Sharon and ripped her mantilla from her head: I saw her face for an instant, white and furious, before she too went down. The cowed students were carted away crying and clutching legs and arms where the dogs whipped to a frenzy by their near-hysterical handlers had taken hold so fiercely of a calf or wrist that they had to be beaten off with truncheons. It was over quickly. In a minute and a half or so, the pavement was clear except for shredded posters, one high-heeled shoe, a few crumpled banners, a spreading pool of something, blood perhaps, or simply orange juice spilled from the smashed flask some thoughtful mother had packed for her child that morning, and, of course, old Hilton luckily too high for the dogs. One particularly demented Alsatian wouldn't give up, leaping for him again and again and falling back, only to leap again like he was attached to some invisible spring yanking him upwards, and snapping at Hilton's bare soles as if he were a treed cat, until his handler pulled the beast away.

Swanepoel came back. He glanced up at the window. 'From your little paw marks I see you've discovered the peephole. Well, what do you think of the latest gimmick?'

I told him it wasn't a gimmick. 'I know Hilton. This is serious. He's out to sacrifice himself.' I told him about Hilton's impatience with theory. This was precisely the action that he, Swanepoel, had been waiting for. For good measure I told him about institutional alienation. I quoted Lestrade on radical orphanhood. 'Hilton has been frustrated too long. Now he's going to make something happen.'

He looked pained. 'How does walking around in your underpants help? This is only one step up on your placard, Barabbas. Another joke, another game.'

'Game? I saw the game you played out there. The dogs, the sticks . . .'

He nodded gloomily. 'Exactly. Toys. If we'd been serious we should have shot the lot.'

Anger made me reckless. 'Why didn't you?'

He stared at me furiously. 'How could we? We're all on the same side. We're all so damn, so damn – ' he searched for a word and when he got it out I knew he'd been listening to my lectures, but knowing made it worse ' – *booshwah*! I mean – take that cross. What's it made from?'

It was my turn to shrug. 'What does it matter?'

He grabbed the iron bedstead and rattled it angrily. 'You've gone to sleep in your cage, man! Of course it matters. It's made of pine, see? And do you know what happens to local pine when it gets wet? It warps, natch. A shower of rain and that piece of lucky-packet carpentry will fall down. But then it wasn't built to last. That mad bimbo van Fölter doesn't plan to be up there long. The way he had calculated it, we'd foam at the mouth and arrest him – but if not, well then his friends'll nip along after dark and take him down.'

'That's a lie.' I showed all the dignity I could muster. 'Besides, how are his friends going to help him? You've got them all locked up.'

He gave a bitter little laugh, half a sob. 'Oh, yes, we locked them up. We packed them, see? Six to a four-man pen licking their wounds, kids retching, old hands up on the top bunk because they know the air's a bit fresher there when the slop pails begin to fill up, when kabam! the usual invasion hits us. Usual but for its size, that is: mommies and daddies, hundreds of them it seemed, fancy folk, togged up to the nines in gold trouser-suits and hacking-jackets and navy blazers, just like yours there, and as per usual crying and shouting all at once and the road outside the station is jammed solid with their cars – oh, I've seen it a hundred times, only tonight it was virtually a riot. News has spread, you see, that we'd put in the dogs. Some parents arrived with bandages, entire damn first-aid kits, and one old lady, tall blonde in a black mink, thick as thatch, comes in, cool as you please and tells the desk sarge he's got to clear the road outside otherwise the private ambulance she's ordered can't get through!' Swanepoel gave a shout of laughter at the memory; he teetered between horrified incredulity and outright amusement and clearly enjoyed it. He leaned an elbow casually against the top bunk muttering and shaking his head at the amazing memory. 'Well, I went outside with the sarge to take a look. Jeez! I tell you I haven't seen so many Rovers and Jags and Lincoln Continentals since I drew duty as parking attendant at the governor-general's garden party there by the Union Buildings – actually I was lumbered, on account of old Wynand Ferreira, who was supposed to be my relief, having to play an away-game that Saturday, for Police Seconds against Benoni Pirates – anyway, as I was saying, there's this crowd of idle rich queuing to bail their brats out of the lock-up, poor little Doreen, and his darling Julius who is delicate, and baby Stuart who never in his life did anything worse than steal sweets from the corner cafe, and boys will be boys, and you're only young once, etcetera . . .' He sighed and stomped around the cell muttering to himself and plunging his hands deep into his pockets and grabbing the linings so that his heavy serge turn-ups lifted inches above his boots. 'That's typical! Par for the course. You nice liberal guys go around being kind to Africans, stirring up trouble, having more fun than an intervarsity rugby match and then at the end of the day, when all hell breaks loose, off you go, home to silk sheets and Mommy's cooking, leaving old Swannie to hold the fort.' He turned on me suddenly. 'Why are you still here? Why haven't your folks been along looking for their little Barabbas?'

I felt deserted, wretched and my voice wouldn't rise above a whisper. 'I don't have any people. I'm from the boy's home. St Joseph's – you know, the one on the Ridge.'

Swanepoel smashed his fist into his palm. 'You're an orphan? Who is going to bail you? Without bail, you'll stay here until the trial. The others will also come to court but they'll pay admission of guilt fines. Can you pay? If you can't – then zap! – STRAIGHT INTO JAIL.'

I tried to keep a grip on myself. 'That's what you want. Look on the bright side,' I suggested in a voice made hideously squeaky by fear. 'We haven't all walked out on you. I'm still here. So is Hilton.'

'For how long?'

'To the end.'

Swanepoel smiled a sarcastic smile that pulled his lips into a thin, tight loop, like one of those rubber seals for stopping preserve jars. 'You believe that, Barabbas?'

I nodded.

'Did it ever occur to you that maybe you aren't an orphan, after all. Maybe your folks simply gave you away because you were too stupid to keep?'

After he'd gone I climbed up to the window. Hilton hung heavily and the last of the sunset was flaring in his hair. It would have been very dramatic if it hadn't been clear, even through the foggy glass, how much he was suffering. Even with the useful little standing support at the foot of the cross the strain on his muscles and circulation must have been excruciating. His head lolled rather dreadfully and his knees were turned out and bent as if he was trying to draw them up, but the ropes or straps stopped that. I'm ashamed to confess I was reassured. He was still there, like me, hanging on.

When Swanepoel arrived with supper of sausages and mash, and stood over me while I forced it down he was suddenly a changed man. He pointed out that by covering my slop pail with my blazer I would 'keep down household odours', and he was quite dismayingly friendly. He made me eat every last bit because, he said, he didn't want me 'wasted away' when I got out. He relished my look of goofy astonishment. My God, but he lapped it up! I didn't care. I begged him to explain. Grinning, he took off his cap, sat down on the bunk beneath me. He told me he had every reason to believe, to hope, that Hilton wouldn't last the night.

'But how do you know?'

'Been out there with the police surgeon. Old van Fölter has got the spastic jitters. The doc says he'll croak by morning – of something fancy . . . car-box-y-hemia.' He said it lovingly.

'What's that?'

'Oh, cramps, breathing problems, collapse – that's just about the order of play. But don't ask me, I'm no medical man.'

'I just thought since you knew the name . . .'

'I'm a policeman,' Swanepoel said with dignity. 'We're trained to remember details like that. Anyway rejoice Barabbas, because I bought your theory that he's in this for keeps. We'll seal off the street – for his own protection, of course. We'll say members of the public, outraged by his behaviour, have made death threats. So no one can get near him. Then by tomorrow morning we're all laughing. Van Fölter gets to be a hero like he's always wanted. We get van Fölter. The commander loves it.'

I looked at his shining eyes. In an awful way his enthusiasm was catching. 'You've got it all sewn up, then.'

He nodded firmly. 'I think so. The commander also has his doubts, mind you, he's never pushed anything as far as this before. Not used to working things through to conclusions, you might say, guys croaking in the streets, and that – but to his credit, he's prepared to let me have a go – 'nothing ventured, nothing win, old Swannie,' was the way he put it. And if we pull it off, it'll be a feather in his cap, a big catch, van Fölter dead that is. As a university man, you get the thinking behind this.'

I did. 'If you land the big fish, you can afford to throw the little one back?'

'It must be wonderful to have an education,' he said.

He showed no sign of wanting to leave. In fact, he settled back on the lower bunk with a contented sigh and stretched out his legs and startled me by actually asking me to tell him some more about 'all the political mumbo-jumbo'. He insisted I called him Swannie – at least, 'between ourselves'. What could I do? I told him about the 'flat-map' theory of African history, I told him about the dialectics of protest. But I must confess my heart wasn't in it. If he noticed my lack of fervour he didn't mention it and when I'd finished he thanked me, jumped up, punched me playfully on the shoulder.

'You're a lucky guy, Barabbas. Not king me to tell him some more about 'all the political mumbo-jumbo'. He insisted I called him Swannie – at least, 'between ourselves'. What could I do? I told him about the 'flat-map' theory of African history, I told him about theere.'

'You really think Hilton is going to die?' It wasn't clear to me whether I asked the question for information or reassurance.

He favoured me with a large, careful wink. 'He'd better. We all depend on it.'

I'd like to say I never closed an eye that night. In fact, I went out like a light and slept like a baby. It might seem heartless, but, the truth is I believed in Hilton – I really believed. Accordingly, it took me some time to get my mind into gear when, early the next morning, with the cold light of dawn pushing through the dirty window, Swanepoel shook me awake.

'Sorry, hey, Barabbas. They sent in the cavalry.' His smile was ghastly.

'Has Hilton been moved?'

He shrugged. 'We refused to lift a finger. The commander told them they'd have to make their own arrangements. Why don't you shin up to the window and take a look?'

Through the dirty glass I watched the whole show. Hilton slumped on his cross with his head still lolling dreadfully. He didn't move. Perhaps he was dead. I rather hoped that he was dead. Death seemed infinitely preferable to any other destination just then. A squad of black workmen, shouldering assorted tools in neat blue overalls, swung into view, two abreast, moving at the double and behind them, shouting out the step, loped a white man in khaki shorts and a broad-brimmed bush hat with a leopard-skin band that matched Hilton's underpants. Clearly he was the foreman and he drove them to the foot of the cross where they marked time with great precision.

'They're about to move him,' I told Swanepoel.

'Who've they got?'

'A gang of workmen. Professionals. Plenty of tools. And big red letters stitched to their backs. DPR, I think.'

He grunted. 'Parks department. The pull those people have got is bloody incredible. I mean who else could just rustle up a working party from the Department of Parks and Recreation at the crack of dawn? It's not right. Makes you realize they've got the country in their pocket. Makes you think.'

The foreman halted his workmen, produced a folding camp stool and sat down while someone ran up a ladder and gave Hilton a quick inspection. There was a hasty conference. I guessed that the chains or whatever had been used to secure him to the gates presented a problem. A man was despatched and returned with a hacksaw. Minutes later the chains fell away and the cross with its deathly pale burden was lowered gently on to the shoulders of the workmen who formed up to take its weight, three beneath the upright and three along the horizontal traverse bar, and then they were off, stamping a right foot in unison as they went and singing, in the way Africans will when a group must work with precision at some heavy job, with the foreman trailing behind, folding stool slung over his shoulder.

'I made a plea to the commander. The bimbo in the underpants wants to die. Let him, I said. The orphan wants to leave. Let him.' Swanepoel sat next to me and patted my shoulder clumsily. 'Make a stand sir, I said, it's your choice.

'He just looked at me with these cow eyes and says: I got no choice, Swannie. Van Fölter's girl did the damage – the one all dressed up like a Spanish granny in black veils and whatall. Late last night she slipped past the constables sealing off the street. Don't ask me how. They got her but she had time to get close to the cross. She swears she heard the crazy bimbo talking to himself. She says he was asking for his old man. So she hotfoots it to daddy and he rolls up and leans on the commander. I mean, he's some big-shot on the airways. He's got government connections as long as my arm. He appeals to the commander as a family man, father to father, y'know. Made me want to puke. Hilton has always been a high-spirited lad, he said, and they have had their little tiffs, as witness the fact that the little beggar hasn't spoken a word to his old pa for donkey's years. He offers a deal – let the commander allow his son's release and he will personally guarantee that the foolish young chap goes away, out of the country, for a long holiday – some place overseas, I don't know where – Belgium? The Bahamas?'

'Bermuda?'

'That's it. I'm sorry, Barabbas. Things don't look too good for you. I've thought about it, inasmuch as an uneducated bugger like me can be said to think – and things don't look too good. So far as I can see there is only one bit of hope . . .'

I felt a faint, foolish surge of hope. 'For me?'

He laughed gently. 'You're joking. I admire a man who can keep his sense of humour at a time like this. No, for me. Like I've told you, I've had enough games. I've had enough of nothing happening.'

I turned over on the bunk and buried my face in the harsh mattress and hoped very much Swanepoel would go away. But I heard him walking around the cell clicking his fingers.

'No, this hope of mine has to do with the talks we been having, you and me. Private like. Now, just look on the bright side, as you told me. Or, put another way, not one door opens but another closes, or something like that. Anyway, what I'm saying is that you having to stay on here now, maybe for ages still, is just what the doctor ordered. I mean, like I said last night – you've got the theory and I want to see action. Right? So being cooped up like this, the *two* of us, you are perfectly placed to tell me all I want to know about how to do it.'

The guy was driving me crazy. 'Dammit man – tell you what?'

He came over and put his lips right close to my ear. 'How to smash the system,' he said.

So, for what it was worth, I told Swanepoel what I knew. He listened very carefully and then proceeded to tell me what had to be done if meaning was to be restored to words such as 'radical' and 'orphan' and the movement towards reality to begin. Soon afterwards he arranged that I should be released on bail which he paid, a fatherly thing to have done though he was too discreet to mention that fact, a tactfulness for which I was grateful. A week later, charges against me were dropped.

I went back to the campus. Swannie stayed in the force. On the face of it nothing seemed to have changed. Admittedly, once back at university it would be fair to say that because of my experiences, I cut something of a figure though I hasten to add that I did nothing to encourage the fame which association with Hilton's last days had brought upon me. In fact I did everything possible to emphasize the great difference between our life styles and political views. I attended classes religiously, passed my examinations, wore my hair very short and never appeared in public without a jacket and tie. It would be fair to say that I was a model student. I insisted on a similar reticence among my followers; one might be known, but on no account was one to be noticeable. Of course, no one had the least idea that I had attracted followers. No one knew we existed, but our group grew steadily and numbered some two dozen after a period of careful and highly selective recruitment. Swannie's cell at the station was growing too and more and more of the junior officers had, as he put it, 'come across'. The third force which Swannie had planned for was growing. The movement towards reality was underway. Sooner or later something was really going to happen.

Hilton was gone but not forgotten. In his absence his followers rallied around Sharon on whom his mantle had fallen. They still talked of revolution, of sacrifice, of solidarity with the oppressed, or praxis and the flat-map theory of history and sometimes even of Buffy Lestrade. But mostly they simply talked. Sharon was making the most of things. She encouraged the belief that Hilton was watching over them like a dead hero among the gods in Valhalla. She had been heard to compare herself with the widow of the assassinated President Allende of Chile. Hilton himself continued to recuperate in Bermuda and nothing had been heard from him since he left.

Hilton's father continued friendly with the station commandant and that was how Swannie heard that his son was secretly planning to return, a reformed character, full of good sense and the right political attitudes. It was decided that we should immediately hold a special session of our action committee. An important decision was taken. Swanepoel and his people were to prepare the station hot-heads for a most violent demonstration. My followers were to whip up the campus in anticipation of a triumphal entry into the city. In this, I think it is fair to say, we excelled ourselves. A few hours after we broke the news, Hilton's return was being compared by his delirious followers to the triumphal entry into Jerusalem. Sharon, ever quick to learn, decided the comparison was so apt that she went out and hired a donkey.

When Hilton stepped off the plane from Bermuda his followers mobbed him and having imagined he was slipping into the country unnoticed, he was shaken by the tumultuous reception. He turned very pale and this, together with his off-white tropical suit and dirty cream silk shirt, gave him a wonderfully ethereal air when he was hauled down the gangway from the plane and seated on the donkey for his triumphal entry into the city. I don't think he knew what was happening to him. My people moved amongst the disciples distributing palms. When Hilton protested it was taken for modesty and his hysterical friends wept and beat their breasts and waved their palms in a fury of adoration. We had planned the route carefully and the march took Hilton past the sites of many demonstrations he'd led in the old days, arriving finally at the police station where Sharon, dressed in full widow's weeds, dropped the donkey's lead and laid a wreath. The policeman inside the station looked on in a fury. The disciples screamed and fainted. Hilton was persuaded to address them. Trembling he was helped down from the ass. The instant his feet touched the ground all hell broke loose. His followers tried to rip down the heavy cast-iron gates across the mouth of the sacred alley. The police came down on them like wolves.

It was never known who struck Hilton down. Each side blamed the other. The fact was he was dead. Having survived his crucifixion, his resurrection finished him. He'd gone to a place where his father's connections could not touch him. Hilton had finally hit back. Reality was beginning to set in.

Private Parts

'The world,' he observed sadly, 'is like one of those round, black sweets children call nigger-balls; cheap to begin with, as it shrinks it becomes multi-coloured, progressively . . .'

Out of the corner of his eye, he saw Madelaine de Tromp lean back in her chair and sigh, or it seemed to him that she sighed. Certainly he saw her write down the remark. She appreciated his aphorisms, he was sure of it, and the remainder of his tutorial would be given over to eliciting another sweet sigh from the prettiest, brightest student in his small class on 'Calvin's Geneva'.

'Our craving for the world's sugary confections, liberalism, false humanism, racial integration, is insatiable and will ruin us as surely as the sweets he desires rot the child's teeth. Tainted desire is the root of evil and we suffer not only because we deserve to but because we desire it . . .'

The university expected its senior lecturers in theology to preach as well as teach. As the only full *dominee* in the department he felt he could hardly have done less. He regarded his job as a living ministry. He was no dry academic; he officiated in the churches of friends whenever he was invited and was even prepared to carry his faith into the smoky staff canteen with a genial, unremitting determination some of his colleagues found infuriating. Pretorius, from engineering, a special enemy, a loud man with hair cut so short it bristled in layers like a bottle brush, and meaty lips, declared him 'too bloody holy to live'. And when someone suggested asking him to the staff dance, Pretorius scoffed that he wouldn't have known what to do with a woman 'even if she was handed to him on a plate . . .'

'Dangerous times, odd weather, personal disappointments are all part of His plan. Not something to be depressed about, or to try and magic away, like savages. Depression is a lack of faith. We trust. We are flotsam in the play, in the current of His will. If we can't build heaven on earth, we can try to rebuild Geneva.'

He heard Madelaine sigh, there was no doubt about it and out of the corner of his eye he saw her pick up her pen and note his words with an approving smile. She was the only student who showed any grasp of the subject and he had persuaded her to write a special paper on the role of civil government in Calvin's Geneva as the model of a Christian state. She wrestled with the *Institutes* late into the night, she told him with evident pride in her stamina in tackling that formidable book. With her blonde hair and glowing, scrubbed, sunburnt skin, in a plain white dress, flat white shoes, no stockings and no make-up she was the woman God had intended, wholly unaffected by the fashions creeping on to the campus, taking hold even of the theology department as he noted with distaste during his lectures to classes of younger students. Many of the boys were allowing their hair to grow and among the few girls taking his courses he became aware of a tendency to do things to their skirts, shortening them, and, when he complained about this, letting out the hems again but tightening the fabric suggestively around the hips. Only Madelaine remained inviolably neat, the woman God had made her. He noticed again her shapely forearms the flesh firmly packed beneath the bronzed skin and admired the small, capable hand sending the pen back and forth across the page of her notebook. When she stopped writing suddenly and found him looking at her, he was embarrassed and walked to the window and stood peering out through the venetian blind. He would have so liked to do something, anything, for her and longed to be able to tell her. But she was pretty and self-sufficient and outside lectures he knew she never gave him a second thought.

The rain had not stopped but the sky appeared lighter and he had a rare view of the campus spread out below his window. The university had been established only five years before on a site which had previously housed an army barracks. Many of the original buildings, mostly prefabs of one kind or another, still remained and were used as temporary lecture halls. Until the building of the Central Block the theology department had been housed in one of the large Nissen huts situated near the servants' quarters. Building went on all the time. Great hulks of unfinished concrete towering above the old barracks stood open to the sky, rearing up across the flat, treeless expanse that was the campus. Huge squares of churned-up mud marked out with rope strung on iron stakes, littered with builders' debris, represented the spacious lawns, the patios and esplanades which one could see in the artist's impression of the futuristic campus to come, on display in the foyer of the Central Block, the only building thus far completed. For a long time now rain, hail and high winds had made work difficult, and when the weather grew particularly bad the builders would pack away their tools and go home. When it improved they would be back to repair the damage done in their absence. Great stretches of the campus were permanently under water. On bad days, the landscape was reminiscent of the battlefields of the First World War during which his father had died fighting for the South Africans at Delville Wood. The suggestions of war were reinforced by old cannon, equestrian statues, flagpoles, barbed wire and other martial relics of the old army barracks still awaiting removal.

There was far more to this weather than the meteorologists allowed. They took the familiar, secular view that there was a scientific explanation. They produced figures which proved that the average annual rainfall was really no greater than that of the past fifty years. But he knew better. The extraordinary weather conditions had continued far too long in what was known to be a climatically stable area for him to be without his suspicions. Sometimes it cleared, the sun came out and shone in a blue sky. But then, when it seemed everyone least expected it, the wind would whip up, swaying the giant cranes and the black clouds would roll back. Of course there were explanations to be found if one looked for them. There was the atomic research station nearby; and radioactive dust drifting over Africa from the French nuclear tests had beautifully coloured the sunsets in the area for years past. A combination of these features satisfied the credulous when they looked for explanations of deteriorating weather conditions and, especially, of the rainstorms.

The storms, although severe, were never prolonged. Progress was being made and eventually the artist's impression would become a reality. But he was not credulous. He set no store by the incomprehensible bulletins issued by the meteorological bureau. Superstition is superstition, he knew, even if science chooses to dignify it. He attended none of the frequent services held to pray for an end to the rainstorms although he knew that by his absence he risked scandalizing his colleagues. Khoury, the Lebanese who taught accounts, lifted his expensive flashy tie off his shirt-front to hide his giggle and dubbed him 'the old maid'. The name had stuck.

'. . . a signal lack of faith in God,' he repeated, 'this fawning on an old fuddy-duddy. It is not the way a free man worships his Maker!' He turned to face Madelaine again.

'People get frightened,' Madelaine spoke with typical gentleness.

'It is the essence of our faith to believe that God holds us in the palm of His hand and does with us what He will. Our very existence here on earth depends upon His merciful dispensation. Consider that, Madelaine, and then ask yourself what business it is of ours if the heavens fall and chaos comes again, if that be God's plan.'

'Still, I'd be frightened if that did happen,' she persisted. 'The heavens falling. On me. It would feel like my business.' She shivered.

'Then pray help is at hand,' he said trying to keep his voice steady.

'Doesn't the *dominee* think that it's really only natural to look for signs and wonders, to be impressed by the more theatrical side of nature? Atmospheric disturbances, for instance? I believe it's a scientific fact that the presence of static electricity before a storm affects human behaviour.' She often used the respectful third person form of address which had made him warm to her from the start. The other students seldom did and sometimes, fresh from other lectures, addressed him with the offensively secular 'sir'.

'Heathens, perhaps, and Catholics and scientists may believe that. But not the true Calvinist. I should be very surprised if he gave way to superstitious nonsense of that sort, and if he started to organize services of thanksgiving or supplication in the vain hope of preventing such phenomena, I should doubt his faith.'

'Yet these prayer services are merely ways of signifying

your human helplessness. Surely our faith rests on our recognition of the power and majesty of the Lord, indeed on our fear of God?'

'Certainly, my dear child. But we do not seek to placate the implacable Judge as if he were a pagan idol by beating our breasts and crying *mea culpa* as the Romans do. If we feel that he is angry with us, we are free to reproach ourselves and seek out the causes for His anger. But to try and turn away His wrath by offering prayers and observing omens is specious, not to say useless.'

Madelaine was making rapid notes.

'After the Fall, God confronted our first parents in the Garden and they tried to run away. But where could they run? He was all around them. Confronted with their shamelessness, they took leaves and covered their private parts. Think about it. From whom were they hiding themselves? Not from their Maker, who sees everything. Of course not. They hid themselves from human eyes. To this day, some things are better concealed.'

The bell rang. He stood up. The students shuffled bags and papers together. Madelaine looked thoughtful. She would go away and try to relate what he had said to Calvin's writings, and mark relevant passages in her bible for discussion. She was the last to leave. At the door she paused. 'Then is there nothing we can do?' she asked.

'If you mean – can we help ourselves? – then the answer is no. We can only pray that our lives reflect His will. But, then, if we can't help ourselves or escape our Fall, perhaps we can help each other.' He touched her gently on the head. 'In need, soul calls to soul.' Her brilliant smile flared and for a moment he almost believed she had understood the deeper meaning beneath his words, that they had a special bond between them and they existed on another, spiritual plane, special creatures, soul mates. But then she was gone and as he watched her hurrying down the corridor to catch up with the other students, he knew it was all in his mind. But he wouldn't give it up, his vision, foolish or not. Pretorius of engineering, it had been reported to him, complained that it was a nonsense for Madelaine to take his course when she had an exceptional mathematical mind. The 'old maid' couldn't make her a priest, however well she did, whereas he could have made her an engineer. In his opinion she was wasting her mind on theology and her beauty on a dry old stick 'who wouldn't know what it was if it bit him'.

His house was a mile or so from the university. He arrived home as the last raindrops were dying on his windscreen. A tea tray waited in the sitting room, conveniently placed on a low table beside his armchair. His maid, Grace, had instructions to put on the kettle when she heard his car in the drive. He took off his coat and boots, settled himself in his chair and closed his eyes.

When he opened them, Grace was bending over the tray, teapot in hand. He blinked. He had not heard her coming. The backs of her knees were smooth and honey-coloured with a sheen on the tautened skin. Grace's dresses, as befitted the maid of a minister, were of a length that ensured modesty. But stooping had the effect of raising her hem several inches, like a curtain. The sight made his heart beat faster. He remembered the day he had come upon her naked in the shower. The door was half open and he deliberately spied on her. He had gone into the backyard to investigate a blocked drain which caused pools of grey, soapy water to gather near the servants' quarters. She had soaped herself thoroughly before stepping under the rusty nozzle and fat white suds were sliding down her back revealing the slick dark skin underneath, shining and new like someone reborn. He could not move terrified as he was that she might see him. He was haunted by the memory. Innocence, he decided, was a terrible cross.

Grace had come to him at a time when he was feeling the strain of keeping house without help. She simply arrived one morning and presented herself in the way of potential servants. She had no references but she professed herself able to cook and she looked clean and neat. She showed no concern when he gave her to understand that he would tolerate no drinking, pilfering, smoking or male visitors and warned her that he arrived home at all hours of the day and would soon find out if she was not doing her job.

She proved clean in her habits, obedient and intelligent. She seemed neither impressed nor perturbed by his status as a teacher and a minister of the Church. She told him that she went to church, meaning, he supposed, the services of one of the sects which proliferated in the cities. Black women, in white robes, their heads covered with white linen cowls, wearing green or red sashes and Star of Zion badges and carrying staves, were to be seen on Sundays gathered in bands wherever they could find a vacant patch of ground. They worshipped in large singing, dancing, clapping circles and listened to lengthy sermons preached by ferocious bearded prophets.

The rain started again, beating steadily on the corrugated iron roof. He drank his tea in silence. Then he leant back and closed his eyes. There rose before him a vision of Grace's knees circumscribed by her modest skirt. To put it out of his mind he tried to recall the morning's lecture. He was proud of the brilliance of his epigrams and of Madelaine's appreciation. But he failed to recover the spirit of excitement he usually enjoyed after discussing Calvin's vision of civil government. He remembered

Madelaine's firm, brown forearms alight with soft golden down. As with his visions of Grace's knees, each detail was so real that he knew how her skin would feel under his fingertips. He opened his eyes quickly. Grace stood before him.

'Excuse me, master,' she said, glancing sideways out of the window as she spoke and clasping and unclasping her hands, 'can master do me a favour? My mother she is very sick.' There was no mistaking the urgency of her voice. 'My cousin, he come quickly from the township. He says my mother is very bad. I must go there.'

Her 'cousin', he had no doubt, was the traditional messenger of sickness, death and domestic tragedies, convenor of funerals, and summoner of dutiful children to ancestral homes; fast-moving, faceless, implacable and infinitely useful.

'Yes, of course you must go to her,' he said decisively. 'Get your things together. I will fetch the car and drive you to your house. Go quickly now.'

'Thank you, master,' she half curtsied and slipped from the room.

He went into the hall and pulled on his boots and raincoat. Then he went to the garage, backed the car out of the driveway and swung it beside the kerb.

Grace was waiting for him, sheltering under a large umbrella in her Sunday walking-out clothes. She carried a bulging paper carrier and black bag, shiny and capacious, the kind which no respectable woman is without, costing little, but capable of carrying anything when the need arises. He gestured to the front seat beside him. He detested the practice common among employers of putting one's servants in the back seat to chauffeur them across town. He had lectured his students against it, calling it cowardly, unchristian, unkind and unnecessary.

Grace gave him a startled look and obeyed. They arranged her baggage on the back seat, her umbrella on the floor and set off. The rain had eased and now fell as a fine mist through which the streetlights showed opalescent rainbows. Grace sat gazing stiffly out of the window.

Feeling the need for some sound other than the swishing of tyres on wet tarmac; he switched on the radio. Its ready voice gave him static and sports news – matches and meetings in provincial hockey, international tennis, horse jumping, polo, cricket and golf: predictions, recriminations, post-mortems bristling with statistics. Lengthy, genial asides soothed and prepared the listener for the long, incoherent interviews which they intercut. With great enthusiasm in a variety of accents players, managers and spectators breathlessly reported the excitements of their chosen contests. There followed sombre news from England. The South African rugby team had lost the test series. The tournament had been marred by the disgraceful behaviour of long-haired, communist agitators who invaded the pitches, hurled missiles at players and spectators, battled with the police causing such chaos that several of the matches had been abandoned or completed only with the greatest difficulty.

The succession of defeats suffered by the Springboks in their national game had depressed the whole country. The violence on the playing fields of England had been reproduced at home where groups of angry sportsmen picketed the British embassy in Pretoria, jostling the staff as they entered the building. The ambassador was mobbed and pelted with *naartjies* until rescued by the police. British airline offices had been attacked. In several Free State towns the queen had been burnt in effigy. Across the country the battle cries of the Boer War were being heard again. There had been reports that survivors of the old commandos were regrouping. The newspapers published pictures of mounted men on secret manoeuvres, slung with bandoliers and powder horns and brandishing muzzle loaders.

He sighed, leant forward and turned down the volume. He wondered briefly if Grace had heard the news. But then rugby was a white man's game, little played by the Bantu, who behaved disgracefully, openly gloating at the defeats the Springboks suffered whenever a foreign team toured the country. Their reaction was childish. But he did not condemn them. The Bantu were childish by nature. He reserved his condemnation for his white countrymen who, as titular Calvinists, at least, should have known better. South Africans played rugby with a zest almost divine. If they had failed, then He had his reasons and it was childish, profane even, to attribute their defeat to any human agency. Giving way to the view that the anti-South African demonstrators attending the tour were evil geniuses, antichrists and so on, as the demonology encouraged by the newspapers and now sweeping the country maintained, was to indulge in superstition bordering on the papist. Like the prayer meetings organized in times of drought in the hope of changing God's mind, these exorcisms were in vain.

It was now quite dark and the rain had stopped. The night, wet, black and pneumatic, swished by. They were nearing the township. He swung off the main road on to the dirt track. There were no streetlights and he couldn't see much beyond the narrow probe of the car's headlights. Occasionally there appeared in the beam groups of men and women suddenly glimpsed in passing on their way home to the township after a day's work in the city, strolling along the side of the road, untroubled by nightfall.

All he could see of Grace was the line of her hair, brow, nose and chin. The few lights did not dispel the shadows on her face as they would have done for a white face, or restore lost tints. The darkness through which they were travelling merely gave way to Grace's more inscrutable blackness.

He recalled the view he had across the tea tray of the backs of her knees. Golden circumferences, radii of delicate creases. He could feel the drops of sweat sliding down his chest. It was as if he could feel the heat of her presence. He had never looked at her the way he had done today. She had never presented him with this view of herself.

There were other aspects. Her round, untroubled face with its full, curved lips seen across the dinner table, behind the floor polisher or the washing machine. He was bewildered by the totality of his recall. Feature after feature rose from his memory with severe clarity: in the shower again, a sheen of water on thighs, hips and calves.

They were passing slowly through the township centre, barely lit and deserted but for a patrolling police van. Shop and office windows were protected by great steel shutters or heavy grilles. Looming up was a large building surrounded by high fences. This must be the school. His sense of direction had gone, even though he had been in the township on occasional Sundays to preach at the church of his progressive friend who organized a Mission To The Townships. On either side of the road the houses crowded together, shouldering each other like spectators at a rugby match for a glimpse of the dusty street, bleak yellow lights trembled behind curtains and over everything hung a giant cloud of smoke, thicker, blacker than any storm cloud, product of thousands of cooking fires, fragrant wood smoke, acrid coal smoke rising to the nose carrying a thousand cooking smells and the pervasive stink of sewage.

He made out the church surrounded by high fences, triangular and uncompromisingly modern, with walls of polished pine topped by a stylized weathercock, half bird, half star. Here he had preached to well-dressed, scrubbed, attentive Sunday congregations and thoroughly enjoyed it. He remembered he was to be there the following day and made a mental note to dig out his sermon draft as soon as he returned home feeling grateful for the familiar landmark. Further up the road he spotted the blue lamps outside the police station glowing gently.

Grace was shuffling her belongings together when suddenly the interior of the car was bathed in light, filling the rear-view mirror and momentarily blinding him. Another car was coming up behind them very fast, its headlights bright. Only when it had passed them did he recognize the grey police van he had seen patrolling the township centre. Gathering up her parcels, Grace thanked him incoherently. He told her not to come back until her mother was better. And then he turned the car around and drove back the way he had come.

He got no further than the church when the headlights of a police van blazed again in his rear-view mirror. He had no way of knowing whether it was the same one that he had seen earlier. Since the police station was located here he supposed that this road must be busy with police vans night and day. None the less, he found himself wishing that Grace had not been sitting beside him when the first van passed. Of course, there was a perfectly innocent explanation for it and besides he was not afraid of the police. No law-abiding man is afraid of the police. But then no one would miss the interpretation which the police might put upon a White man driving at night through a Bantu township with a non-European woman sitting in the front seat beside him.

The police van seemed in no hurry and it settled into a position some thirty yards behind him. He turned into the deserted main street, and, once around the corner, acting on an impulse, he pressed his foot firmly down on the accelerator, covering the length of the street before the police van reappeared in his mirror. As he watched its headlights looming up he realized it was travelling at speed and diminishing the distance between them. Before him lay the darkness of the bumpy dirt track leading to the main road. The police van had resumed its position behind him. He stayed on sixty as he hit the dirt. There was no doubt about it, he was being followed. The wind roared past the windows. The lights of the police van receded, then gleamed again. For a moment he thought that it was slowing down, but a glance at the speedometer told him that he was doing over seventy and the lights were still moving up behind him. He was no longer being followed, he was being chased. Horrid imaginings rose up before him. He saw himself in the dock, the examining magistrate listening intently to the police constable's allegations . . .

He fought to calm himself. If he could outdistance his pursuers by mistake, then perhaps he could do so deliberately. The national road was ahead. If only he could reach it he would disappear into the traffic bound for the city. The needle edged past eighty. Then, without warning, the exterior driving mirror mounted on the car's wing shattered. They were shooting at him.

Before him, through the trees, he could make out the lights of passing cars on the national road. He did not hesitate. He wrenched the car off the dirt and brought it to a violent slithering halt and ran for the cover of the bluegum trees alongside the road. Under the thick cover of the huge trees he followed the road using the headlights to guide him. There was no sign of the police behind him.

The traffic was steady without being heavy. He moved as fast as he could until he had put a couple of miles between himself and his pursuers. Then he stepped from the trees and clumsily began hitching a lift. He had not stumbled more than a few yards along the tarmac when a powder-blue Opel with its radio blaring pulled over on to the shoulder of the road. He ran to it and climbed in, breathlessly muttering his thanks. The car radio concealed the sound of his panting. They were well on their way before he turned and looked at his rescuer. It took him some moments to recognize Madelaine.

'My car broke down,' he managed at last, 'just as well for me that you happened to come along.'

'I've been working in the Bantu township, at the clinic,' she said. 'I help where I can with the unmarried mothers.'

'Good, good,' he hid his astonishment as best he could.

Madelaine nodded. 'These poor women need help. The men won't leave them alone, so they have babies. I don't try to save them – that would be presumptuous of me – but I try to show them how to care for themselves.'

'I had no idea you played such an active role,' he replied weakly.

They drove on. A news bulletin began on the radio. There was more talk of the failed rugby tour of Britain. He glanced at Madelaine. Her hair was loose and hung down over her shoulders. Her arms were bare and her blouse fell away from her neck. He saw her breasts. He glanced down. And looked away perplexed. She wore the shortest skirt he had ever seen. A dark valley ran between her thighs, widening and narrowing as she adjusted brake and accelerator. And in this dress she went each night to the Bantu location! Conscious that he was beginning to sweat, he looked away, rolled down the window and sucked in the air. The radio reported an earthquake in the Western Cape. Many buildings had been badly damaged, some destroyed. Casualties were high. He sank back in his seat. 'Thy will be done,' he murmured to himself.

'Pardon?' Madelaine didn't sound very interested.

'It's nothing.' A little while later, fearing the silence in the car, he said, 'It was a lucky thing you recognized me in the dark.'

'But I didn't,' she said quickly, too quickly.

He no longer felt lucky. But then he shouldn't have spoken of luck. He did not believe in luck. Yet what really hurt was her tone; it suggested that if she had recognized him she wouldn't have stopped at all. Hurt and angry he wanted to hurt her. 'Aren't you rather loosely dressed to be wandering around the African location?' He made a little jerk of distaste with his chin. Even in the half-dark he could see she was wearing lipstick and her perfume was overpowering, like a blow on the head, an attack.

'I dress for comfort,' she sounded sulky. 'The doctor organizing our project advises us to be casual. We don't want these poor African girls to look on us as prancing, superior white madams. He says it's important they see us as women, subject to the same weakness as they are. He's a most selfless man, the doctor. Shall I drop you at home?' She gnawed at her lip. 'I'm not frightened, I have faith.'

At his house he got out of the car with a muttered thank you, tired past caring what Madelaine must think of their meeting, certain only that it was the end of their understanding, if understanding there had ever been. Inside the house he made for his chair and sat down beside the tea tray Grace had not had time to clear away. The police would be busy now tracing the abandoned car. At any moment they would knock on the door. He hadn't the faintest idea what Madelaine had meant when she swore she was not frightened. Quite plainly, she was very frightened of something. So was he. He had been a very great fool.

The night grew colder as he sat in his chair. He hugged his jacket around him. Soon he was dozing fitfully. He dreamed he was walking through the campus on a very dark night. There was rain in the air. Suddenly a search-light set somewhere high up blazed down on him. He glanced wildly about. The dark shapes of the cannon were swinging to centre on him. He began to run and almost as suddenly stopped, remembering the barbed wire perimeter. He woke sweating and shivering and blinking in the overhead light.

It was almost four, too late to go to bed, he decided, and sat down at his desk and pulled out the notes for his sermon hoping that if he were about God's work there might yet be some consolation. Perhaps, somehow, the inevitable visit from the police might not happen until the following day and perhaps, though he did not dare to hope this, perhaps he might still be allowed to give his sermon in the church of his progressive friend in the Mission To The Townships, the very church which had seen the beginnings of his wild, lunatic flight from the pursuing police van. It had been a craven act, he saw that now, on the level of Peter's when he denied his Saviour. 'In fleeing tonight,' he said to himself, 'you have betrayed your convictions, your cloth, your students. You set out to do an act of charity. When challenged, instead of standing up and explaining for all the world to hear that you had brought your maid, in a spirit of Christian duty, to the bed of a sick relative, you denied your duty, your faith and even your lessons to your students and ran like a rabbit.'

He made no headway with the sermon. Quite clearly he was not intended to deliver it. Consequently it was with a feeling of something amounting to relief that he heard the steps on the path and put down his pen and went to meet the punishment he truly deserved.

The police arrived, not in the uniformed phalanx he'd imagined with their grey van snarling at the end of the driveway, but in the solitary person of a fair-haired young man with a puzzled smile who came from the plainclothes CID and produced his identification and apologized sincerely for calling at such a late hour, who was quite abjectly sorry for disturbing a minister on the Sabbath and who was, frankly, 'quite sick to the stomach' at having to enlist the *dominee*'s co-operation on an urgent and distressing matter. His name was Vermeulen and even his handshake, limp and regretful, told of how sorry he was. Vermeulen's apologies were so obviously straight from the heart that by the end of the young policeman's litany, he was so terror-stricken that it took all his willpower to stop himself falling gibbering at the man's feet. With a penitent smile Vermeulen produced from the inside pocket of his grey sports jacket a small photograph. Might he 'impose' on the minister, he wondered, by asking him to say whether he recognized the person in the photograph? It was a picture of Madelaine. She stared out at him with her clear frank gaze, a look he had grown to admire so much.

'But of course I recognize her. This is Miss de Tromp. One of my theology students. What is the matter? Is she hurt?'

'Rest assured, reverend sir, she was perfectly fine when I saw her a little while ago. A little agitated perhaps, but that was probably as a result of my visit. She gave me the photograph.'

'But why? And what were you doing visiting her at this time. It's after four in the morning, man!'

Vermeulen nodded, looking rather embarrassed. 'I say "visit" only in a manner of speaking. Fact is that when the police "visit" someone at this time of the morning it is strictly speaking a raid.'

He jumped up and to hide his confusion marched up and down trying to find something to say, opening and closing his mouth but quite unable to speak a word. His own fear had gone but it had been replaced by a chilling certainty, something terrible was happening to Madelaine.

Vermeulen pretended to study his brown suede shoes. 'We have received complaints. Serious complaints. It seems that there is in the Bantu township a group of volunteers, white women who work under the direction of a local doctor, helping the unmarried mothers. It turns out that Miss de Tromp is one of the volunteers.'

He found his voice then. 'Well, what of it? The illegitimacy rate in the townships is a tragedy, a scandal. I have a colleague in the Mission To The Townships, in fact I am due to preach at his church tomorrow morning – I should say *this* morning – and my colleague tells me that they are a problem of huge proportions, these unmarried mothers. Now, if a group of Christian women try to alleviate the tragedy I applaud them.'

Vermeulen nodded emphatically, but he kept his eyes on his shoes. 'Me too. Good for them, I say. In fact I'd be the first to say so. But you would agree, wouldn't you, sir, that white women entering an African location, besides obtaining permits, legal permission and etcetera, etcetera, are bound to comport themselves in a manner fitting? Not so? Our reports suggest that Miss de Tromp is not so comporting herself. Our reports in fact predict that if she goes on behaving the way she has then she'll be an unmarried mother herself before long. You mention the doctor. Well, it's her relationship with the doctor that forms the basis of the complaint we've had from a number of quarters. The doctor is black, you see. There are witnesses who claim to have seen her leaving his house. This evening. And other times. At night, late at night. You know how serious this is?'

'Of course I know.'

'Well this brings me to my problem. You see Miss de Tromp refused to take it seriously at all. She became abusive. She told me I was too smart by half. She told me that I should get off my high horse because I wasn't as important as I seemed to think. I warned her about her position. It was up to me to decide whether to arrest her. I had the authority. But instead of listening to me she laughed. She said that only God had authority which He passed on to His ministers who in turn invested some of it in officers of the law. Any power I had was only on loan. And she assures me that the minister will confirm this.'

In spite of himself he felt his professional interest quicken. 'Miss de Tromp is a student of Calvin. What she is giving you, in somewhat abbreviated form, is his vision of ideal civil government. But she is largely correct, yes.'

The policeman seemed entranced with his shoes, staring unblinkingly at his toecaps. 'With respect, that is not what I meant. Miss de Tromp tells me that she was never in the township tonight and she can prove it.' The eyes Vermeulen lifted from their profound study of his shoes were hot and bewildered. 'You are her alibi.'

He felt as if a great weight had been lifted from his heart. This was how Lazarus must have realized his freedom. The stone had been rolled away from the tomb of scandal, ignominy and suffering which until then he had seen yawning horribly. He'd escaped the Gehenna into which the enemies of the Church would have tossed his corpse, spat on, jeered at by the world, the butt of lurid headlines and ribald jokes about the minister and his maid, and he had come forth whole. He'd been reprieved, his prayer was answered and Madelaine needed him. Eve called to Adam across the void to save her from the consequences of her sin. He knew instinctively that here was a sign. The Lord's logic. For by providing the alibi Madelaine needed, he also removed the danger threatening himself. If he had been with her all evening then he could not have been the terrified wretch flying panic-stricken before the bullets of the police. There was a beauty to the solution combined with a special kind of hard-headedness, a shrewdness about it that more than hinted at its divine provenance. God was nothing if not practical. By allowing his minister to save the erring lamb he saved himself in a manner free from any suspicion of selfishness, he was not trying to dodge punishment himself, in fact he would suffer for this because the policeman would undoubtedly get the wrong impression, but he could not let that stand in the way of his clear duty to make an act of charity.

'It is true. She was with me all evening. Well into the small hours. I am prepared to swear to that.'

'There'll be no need. If the *dominee* tells me Miss de Tromp was with him then there's an end to the matter. Some things are best kept private.' Vermeulen swallowed hard and gave a small, hopeless smile of apology. 'But I'm afraid I must ask you to account for your movements together this evening. It's a formality . . . but I have to ask.' He blushed deeply. 'What were the *dominee* and Miss Tromp doing tonight?'

'We went for a long drive.'

'In your car?'

'In hers. My car is missing.'

'What?' Vermeulen was suddenly all business and pulled out his notebook obviously happy to find himself on familiar ground. 'When was it stolen?'

He raised a gentle hand. 'I didn't say stolen, I said "missing". Perhaps I lent it to someone and can't remember now. Or someone borrowed it forgetting to ask my permission. In my business I like to take the charitable view and I am happy for the time being to think of my car as missing.'

Vermeulen leaped to his feet and put away his notebook. 'I'm sorry. I thank the *dominee* for his frankness.' At the door he paused. 'Don't worry about your car. I expect we'll find it in that township.'

A spasm of the old fear shot through him. 'Why there?' His voice trembled stupidly and inwardly he cursed his lack of faith.

The policeman shrugged. 'Given time that's where most stolen vehicles turn up eventually. I'm afraid they're pretty knocked about when we get to them. It happens to everything in the township sooner or later. You might mention that to Miss de Tromp next time you go for a drive.' And with a dreadful, conspiratorial wink he was gone. It was a shocking thing to see in a normally apologetic young man.

The insolence of Vermeulen's parting stung like a whiplash. The implications behind that wink enraged him. But then again it was no less than he deserved, it was the price he paid for saving Madelaine and so he bit back his fury and settled down to his sermon again. This time the words came in a rush and he scribbled like a man inspired. When he finished he typed it neatly with a copy for Madelaine. He would read it to her, he decided, and she would hang on every word. Things were going to change. He'd done his part. Now he expected something from her. He expected a great deal from her. Pretorius from Engineering would notice the change, he shouldn't wonder. There'd be less of this talk of his not knowing what to do with 'it', even if 'it' was given him on a plate. And Khoury would discover that he wasn't as old or as maidish as he thought.

Four hours later, bathed, shaved, with a good breakfast in his belly, he stood in the pulpit of the Mission To The Townships church, a few miles from his abandoned car, contemplating the bowed heads of the worshippers. He felt firm, confident. He was in God's hands. He took hold of the polished railings of the pulpit, squared his shoulders, waiting for the congregation to settle themselves, and, conscious that this might be the last sermon he ever preached, he began:

'God is not mocked. Let anyone who doubts the truth of this look at his own life. Can he honestly say that he does not suffer? From sickness, the death of a child, the betrayal by someone in whom he placed his trust? Let him look at the goings-on in the world, the strange and terrible things which afflict all people, and especially our people, at this time. Can he honestly say that God's wrath is not at work?

'Consider the defeats suffered by our rugby players on the infamous British tour. To us, rugby is really our god with a small "g", and to be defeated like that; the mishaps; the players who were injured; it was abnormal. God spoke to us.

'People are sinning against God by these shameful dresses, these barbarous fashions in women's clothing. God took the matter up and He is punishing us.

'The Scripture tells you that your bodies are temples of

the Holy Spirit, and if you sin against your bodies God will destroy you. That is my view. Skimpy women's clothing, mini-skirts, hotpants, these are the outstanding sins.

'The fact is that they disclose the thighs, which are sexually mixed up in a man's mind with the private parts of a woman. If you see the upper thighs of a woman you are struck, sexually struck.

'And the worst part about it is that when these ladies sit next to a man driving a car they can see almost up to their private parts. What man can stand that?

'My main point is that God came from heaven. When Adam and Eve fell into sin, they covered themselves with leaves, they made a kind of mini-skirt; and then God came down and He had animals killed and He took those skins and He made proper clothing for them.

'These barbarous fashions lead to the fact that young men and even older men are sexually disturbed; it makes these men desirous and makes them sin against God.

'God speaks to us daily – if only we had ears to hear Him. God has also spoken to us through this terrible earthquake in the Western Cape, which is a geologically stable part of the world. Property has been destroyed and lives have been lost. Terrible. Thus God claims His own.'

When he arrived home, Grace had not returned. The absence of her attentive hand was everywhere evident. The house was unkempt. The remains of his hasty breakfast cluttered the dining room and kitchen. He had forgotten to close the windows before leaving and his papers – notes on Calvin's vision of civil government – had blown from his study into almost every room. He did not collect them. Instead he turned on the radio. A Bach fugue in all its sliding, metal precision began climbing into the room like an escalator. Good Sunday music.

He sat down in his chair and relaxed. He thought about

Madelaine who must by now be very worried, wondering whether he had given her the alibi she'd asked for. Well, let her worry, he thought. Time enough at his first lecture on Monday morning to enlighten his brightest and prettiest student as to the true nature of things and his expectations for the future; an end to the lewdness, the skimpy dresses, the trips to the location. There was to be an altogether more loving and attentive and respectful attitude towards her teacher and, yes, why put too fine a point on it? – her saviour. He closed his eyes and imagined some of the fresh attitudes as well as some of the new positions in which he would let her show him this respect.

Bach finished and the news came on. It seemed the government had published a bill making it an offence to try and alter the weather without permission. He allowed himself a grim little smile. Weather modification was defined as 'the artificial promoting, accelerating, increasing, aggravating, impeding, suppression, retarding or altering of the natural occurrences of rain, snow, fog, hail or similar precipitation, or lightning, or a tornado or cyclone or similar atmospheric phenomenon . . .' This was superstition run mad. He did not think that the Lord would be very impressed by this new law. Reaching over he switched off the radio and settled back in his chair again. He hoped Grace would be home soon. She would probably be tired after her journey. On Sunday night he never ate much supper. He decided he would tell her that she could leave him to feed himself. She could go to her room. Perhaps, he thought, she would decide to have a shower.

The Kugel

Joel Wolferman came up to university in a powder-blue Porsche, smiled often, spent money, and left suddenly and the manner of his leaving so grievously wounded the student body that the scar is still visible. His time on the campus, when people looked back at it, came to seem a watershed; they talked of life 'before Wolferman' in the way their parents talked of 'before the war'. You could say that the manifestation of Wolferman in university life became, in student terms, the equivalent of the serpent's appearance in Eden. He marked the Fall. After Wolferman an age of innocence was no more; after Wolferman, Eddie Springer, one-time big student leader who had not taken an exam in five years and was definitely the old man of the campus, politically aware, often arrested and widely admired, began to take annual examinations with conventional regularity, to pass them and to become, as everyone knows, an authority on comparative African government with a famous thesis on 'Ethnicity in the Gold Mines', which was later published.

After Wolferman, the kugels (deceptively named, for the sleek missiles they were, from those sweet heavy puddings stuffed with raisins) redoubled their social energies, flashing hungrily across town in their Italian sports cars, stood strategically poised on the library steps sunning their breasts and reactivated the marriage market with a vengeance, hunted down medics, dentists and lawyers-to-be without quarter, and cursed all politicians.

Wolferman got off to an awkward start because he

became so quickly and in so many senses notable. Tall and dark with a mass of black curls and a pointed chin, with eyes of some indeterminate colour, blue mixing with green, 'salted candle-flame eyes', as Judith Klein, one of his disappointed hunters once described them; the new freshman was apparently an orphan yet the fellow clearly viewed himself as being already adult and this daring maturity, this air of authority in a young man who should by rights be all fingers and thumbs, intrigued, infuriated or attracted all who came to know him.

His uncle had sent him up from some remote country town; Ted Malkin found out that Wolferman's uncle had made his fortune by importing cheap labour from the neighbouring states in the north for the gold mines. He'd been a broker in human muscle, as Malkin put it. Wolferman had told him about the beastly trade without the hint of a blush and seemed (Malkin again) to think bloody well nothing of it. Wolferman moved into Malkin's building where students occupied the warren of small rooms on the eight floors; only Wolferman didn't simply take a room, he took the penthouse unused for years and built for the exclusive enjoyment of the entrepreneur who had put up the block, a great place designed for a man with money. Enormous picture windows looking out across the city to the distant flat-topped mine dumps, pale, gleaming yellow in the evening sun, their sides roughened with stubborn climbing grass. Into this place Joel Wolferman moved with great panoply. Ted Malkin in his little bedsitter on the third floor watched it all, saw the huge pantechnicon arrive and the sweating removal men bossed by an Indian with gold teeth carry the new man's things upstairs.

'He arrived with this big van and out of it came more furniture than you need to open a department store, up the stairs he goes at the head of a band of sweating lackeys and proceeds to allow himself to be installed up there on the roof of the world like some great, bloody pasha. Can you believe it? Can you imagine how much that penthouse cost? I met him later, knocking on all the doors and inviting everyone up for a drink. There must have been about a dozen of us, we sat on packing cases and drank whisky. Whisky! We stared at his furniture which is tubular with leather and stared at the view. You could see right across the city towards the gold mines – like bloody executives! He's got these spidery pictures, Eddie, porno pictures, at least that's what they look like to me, drawings, you know, men, women. Everything bloody curling and dangling. He tells me they're going up on the walls. Imagine that; he sat there in this amazing white suit and white shoes, sipping whisky and telling us he intended to hang up these porno pictures on the walls. Bought with the fortune made from selling black man's sweat. And, *no*, it doesn't worry him. Why should it? All this without a blush. What with his weird clothes and all, and his frightfully gung-ho manner, and his views of the gold mines, this guy is too much. You wait until you meet him, Eddie.'

Sturdy, energetic, cheerfully uncouth, stubby-fingered, Eddie Springer with his sharp intelligent face and his lank yellow hair was at the height of his fame on the campus. He'd just been inside, in solitary confinement, and this for the second time, for a full forty-three days and only got out because of the intervention of some smart lawyers his parents had hired in the face of Eddie's protestations. The story was already all over the campus about how he'd been picked up outside the prison gates by his old folks who were just about to drive away when these two security policemen came running out with a big red biscuit tin and in the biscuit tin were all the odds and ends he'd left behind in his cell, his toothbrush, his comb, and his handkerchiefs and these were handed over to them with many salaams and fixed smiles and Eddie's parents had actually gone and thanked the cops feeling tremendously impressed at their kindness. Everyone heard about how Eddie gave them hell for that, saying that they shouldn't have accepted the biscuit tin and certainly should never say 'thank you' to a couple of gorillas, as if they approved of them, paid thugs who'd stood him in a corner for eighteen hours without sleep and threatened to ram a broom handle up his arse and generally given him a hard time. Eddie's parents, the legend went, had snapped right back that that sort of talk was all very well but they didn't really suppose the police enjoyed having to do what they had to do any more than Eddie himself did, but there was after all such a thing as elementary courtesy. That phrase became a catchword among the radical students for a few weeks, and it appeared on a banner in the very next demonstration: 'Elementary courtesy for political prisoners'. All who saw it agreed that it was absolutely rich.

And so it was that when Joel Wolferman came to classes for the first time, Eddie Springer who was strolling in the sunshine with Barney Tembisa, the black medical student, crossed over the road in Samaritan fashion and spoke to Wolferman with a naturalness which was one of his most admired qualities, and even more admirable in this case since Wolferman was wearing a dark blue pin-striped suit, patent leather shoes like gleaming black pools beneath his turn-ups, and a rich red rose in his buttonhole. Passers-by stopped to witness this odd confrontation, the intensely serious Springer in his sandals and old brown corduroys and the strange new man in his amazingly unsuitable suit.

'Wolferman? My name is Springer, students' council, and since you're a new guy here I was wondering how you felt about the issues.'

The new man gave a genial smile. 'What issues?'

Eddie Springer drew Barney forward. 'I have one right here. Barney Tembisa, medical student, third year. A living issue. If the government has its way it will kick Barney off the campus and people like him who aren't white will be packed off to some bush college in the back of beyond, if they're lucky. We're fighting for people like Barney, to keep this university open for people of all races. We're fighting for academic freedom.'

Wolferman reached out and shook Tembisa's hand. 'It must be hard to be a living issue,' he said, carefully polite.

Barney Tembisa was clearly taken aback. Tembisa's looks gave a misleading impression of the man. His rather sad brown eyes and his plump, round, kindly face in which a pair of prominent cheekbones were the only things to interrupt an almost perfect circularity deceived people when they contemplated his white coat and carefully pressed grey flannels; on the one hand he was clearly going to make a fine doctor one day, on the other he was all too likely to end up in jail before he qualified as he made no secret of his ambition to see a total end to the colour bar and the destruction of the government and all its works.

'I'm not an issue in myself,' Barney said.

'He's too modest. If he isn't – who is?' Springer demanded. 'We're fighting a war and you can either join us or you can while away your time on the sports field and eventually be caught by the kugels. The kugels, in case you don't know, are those rich girls with names like Lorraine, and Wanda and Michelle, usually driving Alfa Romeos, whose brothers are clerks on the Stock Exchange or studying to be dentists and whose fathers are rich business men in the shady suburbs; they don't come to university to take a degree, they're here to become known, to look around and have fun and find a husband. A kugel is a sweet, clinging kind've kid, who comes on round and soft like a sugary cake, but is really a kind of hunter killer. You get lots of them here. Usually they have big breasts. It's either them or the issues, Wolferman.'

'And if I don't like the choice?'

'Life is choosing, Wolferman. Have a word with Barney. He'll explain.' And with a burning look, he went on his way.

'Eddie has this thing about big breasts,' Tembisa said, smiling. 'He's prejudiced against them. Maybe because his girlfriend, Belinda, was a kugel with breasts once. But then she saw the light. She was politicized. She runs a crêche for the children of the black cleaners here. As a result, her breasts have disappeared, as it were. They say she wears vests now. Medically speaking that's not possible, but politics can work miracles.' The black man was faintly amused. 'Seriously, Eddie wants to know if you'll run with the kugels or come and join us in the fight against oppression.'

'And you are one of the oppressed?' Wolferman was clearly sympathetic.

Barney nodded slowly. 'I suppose I am.'

Thoughtfully Wolferman sniffed the rose in his lapel. 'I'm definitely against oppression.'

'Well then what do you say?'

Wolferman gave his charming smile. 'Would you like to come to a party?'

Eddie Springer never went to that party. He never went to any of Joel's parties and there were many of them. Barney Tembisa went but then as Eddie said gloomily, he supposed that Barney could afford it, being who he was and coming from where he did. He deserved to go to parties. Lots of other people went to the parties in the big penthouse. The porno pictures on the wall turned out to be drawings by Aubrey Beardsley; the identification immediately made by the fine arts students greatly disappointed Eddie Springer. People fell silent in Wolferman's enormous apartment, gazed at the thick white wall-to-wall carpet, the massive hi-fi, the steel and leather chairs and whispered about the huge four-poster bed, shook their heads over the money it must have cost, and drank his liquor with an enthusiasm which could never quite disguise their sense of disbelief that anyone could really live on this level. Joel Wolferman introduced the students to a taste for enjoyment which dulled political commitment by encouraging a mood of sticky camaraderie. Eddie wondered aloud whether Wolferman was not perhaps a government agent placed on the campus to confuse the issues and weaken opposition. Belinda, Eddie's girlfriend, talked of him as that overdressed, shining fool. Ted Malkin ran his hand through his thick blond hair and blew harshly between his teeth when he mentioned his name, a usual sign of irritability, lamenting the fact that Wolferman lived in the same building.

'I'm just getting in from some demonstration, tired and thirsty and maybe I've been kicked around a bit and I'm walking up the stairs and who comes down, dressed for tennis but not just for bloody tennis, but dressed to the nines as if he was going off to bloody Wimbledon or somewhere, but Wolferman, swinging his racquet with that tally-ho look of his and wanting to know when I'm going to give him a game. It pisses me off, I can tell you, it damn well pisses me off.'

Eddie Springer's mood grew blacker. Damn good

people were getting drunk on Wolferman's booze up in his penthouse. The man was threatening political education on the campus. It was in this mood that Springer confronted Wolferman in the famous 'Who pushed who?' incident. Nobody saw it. All one had was Eddie's account, spoken painfully through bruised lips.

'I said to him quite plainly, I said, your life style spits in the face of decent people, of people like Barney Tembisa. And he answers me, d'you know how he answers me? By asking if I play golf. Did you know he was buying a boat so he can go sailing at the weekends? When he's not playing rugby, or rallying in that ridiculous Porsche. I said to him that playing golf wasn't much use to a black student living in two rooms in the township and expecting to be kicked out of university tomorrow. All he said to that was that golf was a funny game and you never knew until you tried. I reminded him that his money came from his guardian and his guardian got his money from the sweat of black labour, cheap labour, imported to work on the mines, and he couldn't turn his back on that. But that's exactly what he did, telling me he had to go off and play squash and they never kept the courts if you didn't turn up on time and that's when I put my hand out to stop him, that's all I did, trying to get his attention, and that's when he attacked me.'

At his parties in the penthouse Joel Wolferman told a different story: 'Poor old Eddie became too excited and launched himself at me like a terrier. I plucked him off, gently though, before he did himself any harm and put him down carefully. I'm afraid the trouble is that I just don't seem to be able to live up to his expectations.' And people continued to climb the eight flights to his place for the music and the great views across the mine dumps and the endless supply of liquor.

There were a few who talked of converting Wolferman's undoubted energy to the cause, like Barney Tembisa, in whom the activity was regarded as a positively saintly thing to do since he had less need than anyone to try and reform Wolferman. Eddie Springer's girlfriend, Belinda, seeing the effect it was having decided that it was about time she spoke her mind and received permission from Eddie to go to his next party, in the course of duty. Ted Malkin in his tiny room in the third floor had done his bit to help. He complained in writing that the loud music interfered with his studies and he succeeded in getting the landlord to impose a midnight limit on the parties and was extremely upset when he was jeered at the very next time he addressed a student meeting.

'You don't care about academic freedom! About people like Barney Tembisa – all you care about are bread and circuses . . .'

'And parties!' came the merciless rejoinder.

The kugels vied with one another to capture Wolferman. Girls like Melissa Dworkin who had been a rag princess, sister to the famous Clara who had gone to live on a kibbutz and had actually shot an Arab during an attack on the settlement, which caused a considerable stir when news came back since Clara had never shown the stamina needed merely to pass first year sociology. He took Melissa out in his Porsche for 'a drive', but it turned out that 'the drive' was actually a rally and she was along to do some rudimentary map-reading. A few months later Melissa was pregnant by an extra-mural articled clerk only in his second year and had to leave; this tragedy was widely ascribed to the disappointment she'd suffered at Wolferman's hands. Then there was Judith Klein, the once slim, pretty Judith with her fondness for skintight yellow leggings and Mexican ponchos who took him shooting on the family's game ranch in Bechuanaland only to find that Wolferman liked nothing more than to sit up well into the small hours drinking whisky with her father and never seemed to go to bed at all. In the next weeks Judith began eating prodigiously, it was rumoured, and had to be sent to a clinic. Ruthie Shapiro, acknowledged queen of the kugels, got closest to scoring with Wolferman by batting her big brown eyes at him and luring him to her place late at night, slipped away after strategically placing him beside the pool, emerging a few moments later from the changing room quite naked with an invitation to join her in a midnight swim. Wolferman's lightning reaction was to nip across to his car and produce from the boot a costume for each of them, to insist that she put it on, turning his back while she did so and then changing himself while she closed her eyes, then picking her up and repeatedly ducking her in the pool behaving, Ruthie said afterwards, 'like some bloody ten-year-old having a bath with his big sister.' She stopped going to his parties and brooded on her humiliation.

Then Eddie's girlfriend, Belinda, spoke her mind, marching up to Wolferman in her black stretch slacks and her plain white blouse through which could be seen very faintly the straps of the vests she was said to wear, and fixing on him her large blue eyes which bulged just a little but not unattractively, she demanded to know whether Wolferman was deliberately trying to subvert and destroy student opposition to government policies. Wolferman replied that he hoped very much that he had done nothing to injure his fellow students of whom he was tremendously fond. Belinda told him to prove it. Wolferman promptly asked her out to dinner and Belinda was so angry she accepted. He took her to the Mediterranean, the smartest nightclub in town. She sat in the pink plush chair pale with rage and shame and would eat only a little clear soup, a piece of bread, a single piece of ham and she toyed with a glass of wine while she was obliged to watch Wolferman work his way with great expertise through the choicest dishes on the menu. His lobster alone, she computed, cost enough to keep a whole family she knew in the African location in powdered milk for at least a week and then something or other with truffles which followed would have subsidized a soup kitchen. She contained herself in the restaurant but on the way home she'd made him stop the car and threw up on the side of the road. Eddie thought this was a wonderful way of expressing the nausea she must have felt. He called a special meeting of the students council.

'The time has come to cut Wolferman out.'

'It will be no good if it's just the politically aware people who stay away from his parties,' Belinda said. 'As long as the kugels keep going they attract all the men.'

'Then we must persuade them to stop,' Eddie said. 'Maybe that won't be too difficult. The kugels are getting just a little pissed off with Mr Joel Wolferman because they reckon he's playing them around. He won't declare himself for them just as he won't declare himself for us. If we combined to freeze him out I reckon we could hurt him. I mean a guy who comes to university has got some obligations, for God's sake. He's got to attend to the way things are. He can't go on doing as he damn well likes.'

'If we can cut him out, it'll really hurt,' Belina agreed. 'What's clear about Wolferman is he likes to be liked. You can feel it.'

'Maybe we should give him a last chance,' Barney Tembisa suggested.

Ted Malkin patted the black man's shoulder. 'Barney, you're too damn kind. If anyone is entitled to put the boot into the likes of Wolferman, it's you. Here you are poor and black and coming from the township with nothing and there's Wolferman with his fancy suits and his whisky always living it up and throwing his money about and you can still ask us to give him a chance. It's generous. More, it's damn generous. But it's time for generosity to stop.'

'Did you know that Wolferman is going around saying that racialism doesn't matter to him? He doesn't care about it,' Eddie demanded.

'It's true. He told me in that awful nightclub that he feels nothing about colour,' Belinda confirmed.

Barney smiled ruefully. 'Somehow I don't think that's what he means.'

'Then he should say what he means,' Eddie Springer declared.

Barney shook his head. 'He won't understand why we're doing this.'

The others fell silent in the face of Tembisa's extraordinary tolerance. Belinda gave Barney an agonized look.

'Look Barney,' Springer said gently, 'let's say that we're actually helping him. How else will he understand that he's got to choose where he stands on the issues?'

'But Eddie, don't you see? He doesn't care about issues,' Barney shook his head. 'He's got other, well, feelings. There's love in him Eddie.'

'Love's for kugels. This is war,' Eddie said. 'He has set himself.above us. All of us – kugels as well as radicals and it's in the interest of the whole student body that we take action. Love's all very well but this is a question of principle, as I'm sure Barney would agree. I am going to have a word with Ruthie.'

Here began a period of rare amity on campus, proving, as people said, that when the students felt themselves threatened they would band together, sink the differences between radical and kugel and present a united front. In the meeting between Eddie Springer and Ruthie Shapiro a bargain was struck.

A few days later Wolferman came looking for Eddie Springer on the campus. He was pale and for once, Springer noticed with satisfaction, he wasn't smiling.

'I think I'm the victim of some sort of conspiracy, Springer.'

'Something like this had to happen.'

'What is it exactly that I'm supposed to have done?'

'You haven't understood the way we are. Everything you do, the way you live, deliberately rejects everything we believe in.'

'All I've done is to give a few parties.'

'There's more to life than parties – or golf,' Eddie said, remorselessly sincere.

Wolferman sighed. 'What can I do?'

Eddie sighed a measured sigh he really enjoyed, deep enough for sympathy, long enough to allow him to order his thoughts. 'Well I suppose once upon a time something might have been done, a few protest marches, or a couple of lunchtime demonstrations. Could be that had you even found yourself a kugel it might have helped, but you've gone your own way.'

Wolferman said nothing for a time. He just stood there shaking his head. 'I ask people to my place and no one comes.'

'I warned you, Wolferman.'

'Look Springer, I tell you what, if it will help I'll come on a march.'

Eddie gave an incredulous yelp of laughter. 'I appreciate the offer, but the time for that has passed.'

'Then I'll find myself a kugel,' Wolferman's face was set and serious.

'Sure,' Eddie grinned encouragingly. 'Why don't you try and do that.'

Wolferman seemed prepared to ignore the grinning scepticism with which this encouragement was delivered. 'Okay, I will,' he said.

From that time he was never seen again on the campus. Ted Malkin reported that he'd confined himself to his penthouse. There was something faintly alarming in Wolferman's voice, worrying enough to send Eddie to firm up the alliance with Ruthie who said that she was ninety-nine per cent certain that her girls would hold out against any attempt on the playboy's part to break the boycott. Of course she wasn't saying it could never happen. Her people were only human. But at the moment they were as fixed in their desire to make Wolferman sweat as the radicals were. If he did tempt someone, it would have to be one hell of an offer, Ruthie said, immediate marriage and a Greek honeymoon, at the very least . . . Eddie Springer came away grateful for her powerful reassurance.

It was surprising, then, how well Eddie took the news a week or so later that Wolferman had broken the blockade. Ted Malkin overheard someone climbing the stairs to Wolferman's apartment in the early hours of the morning.

The other radicals took it badly. The kugels had betrayed them. It was another Munich, Belinda said and reduced Ruthie Shapiro to tears by heckling her in the canteen with shouts of 'Peace in our time!' and 'Chamberlain!' They were nonplussed when Eddie simply smiled and told them not to worry.

'Don't sweat. We've got the boy boxed in. He can't win now, whatever he does. The big spender with the parties and the view of the gold mines is cut down to size. *Wunderkind* is washed up.'

'You mean that the god has left him,' said Ted Malkin, literary as ever.

'Right. From now on he's just another guy who has been hooked by a kugel.'

'What now?' Belinda demanded.

'That's easy,' said Eddie, 'now we find out who she is. The very next time Ted reports activity in the penthouse we will be ready.'

When the call came Eddie and Belinda moved into Malkin's room. The idea was to keep vigil around the clock; whenever it was that the lovers emerged from their nest the stairs were their only exit and passed Ted's room where the reception committee would be waiting for them.

It seemed as if Wolferman and his kugel had no intention of coming out. Two days and nights passed and no one left the penthouse though several scouting expeditions reported that an ear pressed to the door detected signs of life within. The siege continued.

On the third night, about four in the morning, the secret watchers were shaken by a thunder of boots on the stairs and ran to fling open the door in time to witness a group of uniformed policemen tearing up the stairs, whooping like huntsmen in full cry. One man carried a bright axe in a canvas scabbard. The watchers followed. Other students woken by the noise began emerging from their rooms. Outside the penthouse the policemen paused for a brief council which seemed primarily concerned with deciding who should have the privilege of wielding the bright axe, clearly one of the perks of the job. The council over, and the door breached in moments, the policemen shouldered through the splintered gap followed by the excited students.

Joel Wolferman lay on the big, four-poster dressed in a

pair of blue shorts and a white teeshirt advertising a fund to save the white rhino from extinction. He seemed quite unperturbed, almost as if he had been expecting the raid, lying back with a cigarette blowing smoke at the roof. He was, everyone realized once again, a very big fellow and the policemen approached him with caution but Wolferman offered no resistance. Beside him, beneath the heavy white silken bedspread with the Mexican or Aztec pattern woven in gold thread, lay Barney Tembisa. They lay so still they might have been posing for a picture. Indeed, clearly anxious not to miss the opportunity one of the policemen produced a camera and took several shots.

Belinda was never to forget the white bedspread with its gold, geometrical patterns, or, as a policeman with an expert flick tossed it aside, the black man lying on the white sheets utterly naked. Other students were by this time crowding in to the bedroom with sleepy cries of bewilderment, trying to peer over the shoulders of those lucky enough to have a view. No one spoke. Tembisa was ordered off the bed and as he got out he shot a look of horrible embarrassment at Belinda and scurried across into a corner crossing his hands before him, his large, soft buttocks shaking. He was handcuffed. Wolferman was handcuffed and continued to lie on the bed, smoking, lifting both hands to his mouth.

Without warning Eddie Springer attacked, throwing himself on Tembisa who tried hopelessly with his manacled hands to push him away but Eddie bore him down, punching and kicking him repeatedly until a policeman pulled him off. Wolferman watched from the end of the bed as Eddie's friends dragged him away. Barney Tembisa knelt in the corner, there was blood on his mouth and his shoulders shook. Belinda saw tears course down his cheeks, drop from his lips, run down his chest and disappear into the thick hair of his groin. Wolferman got slowly to his feet.

'Always knew you'd turn up at one of my parties, Springer,' he said.

Downstairs, only Belinda was among the crowd who gathered to watch them being taken away. They were marched out by the policemen into the clear early morning light. Wolferman in his shorts and rhino teeshirt and beside him, Tembisa, who for the sake of decency had been draped in the gold patterned bedspread which was far too large for him and dragged behind him like a cloak. Belinda through her pain and fury recognized something absurdly dignified in the progress of this strange couple, the tall, striding figure of Wolferman and beside him the richly swathed, plump figure of his unlikely queen accompanied by their uniformed attendants, yes, that was it, she thought – despite the fact that, as she explained to Malkin and Springer later, she was no monarchist – there was something hideously regal about the procession of Wolferman and his kugel to the waiting police van.

On the Frontier

Maxie Meyerson ran a chemist's shop on what began as the far edge of town. He'd gone there soon after completing his pharmacy course at College, ten years earlier. He'd chosen this most unlikely suburb because it was raw bush, still practically frontier, and on the frontier a man could earn his whack and he hoped to earn a very big whack indeed. With the small inheritance his father left him he bought the shop, had his name painted, along with his pharmacy degree, on the lintel in wavy white letters and he stocked up.

Meyerson had been very influenced by his father in his decision to live rough but free. On the frontier a man could do anything, Papa Meyerson said, and in Africa, new Africa, such things were possible, even for Peruvians. His father and mother had come to the goldfields of the Transvaal from Poland before the turn of the century when they were still children. They had met and married in Johannesburg where Meyerson's father worked down the mines. They were among those lower-class Jews who had belonged to the Polish Russian Union, and hence the contemptuously inaccurate description of them as 'Peruvians', poor immigrants who worked hard for the big mining bosses, sometimes Peruvians turned Anglican, who appreciated in these Europeans their useful urge to work until they dropped, however menial the role, however poor the pay. When too much dust got into Papa Meyerson's lungs and he quit, his wife Friedle found a job as concierge of a tall, damp, flaking block of flats in the centre of town. When Friedle died old Meyerson took over and dealt with the clamorous tenants, saw to the great hissing patched boiler in the basement and oversaw the fitful energies of the black houseboys who lived in concrete barracks among the chimneys up on the roof of the block. He hired them, fired them, dampened down their continual drink parties and helped to carry out the corpses after the traditional Saturday night parties with their traditional stabbings. As young Maxie lay in his bed he would often hear the screams. The flats were old and dark, and the cooking smells, the cabbage and the onions, had impregnated the woodwork which, in all the flats, was painted a dark green. The walls and metalwork were covered in a heavy, shiny grey.

'When you get big, boy, don't you go and do what I did – don't you go and sell yourself to some fat boss. The people who came from Poland, like your mother and me – know what they did, they came away from the ghetto so as they wouldn't be murdered? Thanks very much. You think that's pretty smart? Don't you believe it, sonny. We left there to stop being murdered and came here to find ourselves committing suicide. Don't go working for nobody, Maxie. You go into business for yourself. This is Africa. Being born Polish and stupid, what we didn't know could fill libraries. But you can do it. You can do anything you like here. It's frontier.'

His father never lived to see the shop Maxie bought with his small sum and a bank loan, just three weeks after completing his pharmaceutical studies. But the old man had left him in no doubt of his belief that he would eventually make it and the purchase of the shop on the furthermost edge of the city was a source of enormous pride to Maxie. When he moved in, it was true to say that he was quite literally confronted by bare veld. There was no other chemist's shop for miles.

But Maxie looked the other way for a moment and progress caught up. Soon ditches and foundations were being dug, trees cleared, and houses were going up and all the red dust was a considerable irritation to Meyerson in his early years because he found it almost impossible to keep his windows clean and he was continually dusting his shelves. When the construction was at last finished he found himself in possession of a chemist's shop right in the middle of an undistinguished white suburb where the mothers sent their kids in for magnesia and aspirins and bicarb, for patented nerve pills, and for laudanum-laced potions with Dutch names used for knocking out the baby when he wouldn't sleep, and liver pills. But business was business and the prescriptions multiplied as the young wives who moved to the neighbourhood became mothers and needed drugs. Prescriptions paid his bills in the early years when his counter trade ran at a loss and the kids came in barefoot and shaven-headed and stole cough-drops and glucose tablets if he dared to put them on his glass shelves in front of the till. They wrestled with each other, two, three and sometimes four of them crammed onto the big green scales by the door which gave your weight for a penny, and he'd rush at them and bowl them out onto the street. But business grew, along with the families it served, and he prospered and he thought sometimes with honest pleasure of the pride his father would have felt.

The natives were something of a problem. He wouldn't turn them away from his store: they were customers like anyone else, and when they had money and he had the goods, why shouldn't he serve them? And he wouldn't fence off his shop into two halves; Meyerson was no racist.

On the other hand he couldn't allow his white customers to be swamped by black men and women off the streets who came in to buy cheap plastic jewellery, or bleaches for their skin, or hair straighteners, or hairpins, or lipsticks. So he instituted a rule that only one African was allowed in at a time. It was an unwritten rule and by and large it was unspoken too, but it was understood throughout the servants' quarters in the backyards of the new houses and it was rare that Meyerson had to ask the black customers to leave the shop and wait in line outside the glass doors.

Meyerson, small, dark, prematurely balding in his late twenties, but full of energy with an incisive, abrupt manner to him, worked very hard, worked, as his father would have said, like a European, living in the two rooms above the shop, cooking and cleaning for himself, slaving for the ten years that it took to repay the loan to the bank. He did not go to the cinema. For recreation he walked. At night he read the trade papers, then went to bed. He didn't like that loan, it smacked of working for a boss, though he knew of course that it was very different; a lot of business men took money from the bank, that's what banks were there for. His friend Michaelis, a fashion buyer, urged him to keep on the loan, saying it was cheaper to service the debt than to eat into his capital in repayments, but Meyerson persisted. The bank wasn't a boss but it felt like one, and so he paid back the debt for his father's sake.

When he paid off the debt, Meyerson expected at last to make his packet. In truth his profits had been growing; this was due in large part to what he called his 'lines'. For Meyerson did not make his money from his prescription charges, or his patent medicines, or his counter trade. He made it by isolating and then promoting some new line.

He got advice about the latest gimmick in the trade from his friend Michaelis, when they met once a month for their lunch in the Railway Hotel. Over the invariable roast beef, Michaelis would tell Meyerson what was on the up and up, what women were after just then. Meyerson handled his promotions with the same energy and enthusiasm which he brought to everything else. One month it would be a new permanent wave. He would hire a hairdresser and a model, set up a chair right there in his shop and demonstrate to his customers the wonderful setting qualities of this new product on which he was making a special offer, for one week only, whilst stocks lasted, and the hairdresser would wash and set the model's hair right there in the shop in front of a small audience of enthusiastic housewives from the suburb, while out on the pavement a group of curious and slightly disbelieving Africans would watch with big eyes through the window. In this way, Meyerson promoted electric hair rollers, herbal cosmetics, and latest aids in chiropody for those with troubled feet, and always with demonstrations, always with expert advice, always with special offers whilst stocks lasted. The interest this provoked amongst his white customers inside, and his black customers outside the shop, increased as time went by. It was amongst one of these excited groups of bewitched Africans that Meyerson first noticed the albino.

He was tall, around twenty, in an old grey felt hat with its broken brim pulled down over his ears and a pair of sunglasses with bright green plastic frames. He was a thin boy and his clothes were old, probably cast-offs, a dirty green sports coat and threadbare, flapping grey flannels short enough to show he wore no socks. It was strange to see this pale, tattered creature prancing around on the cat-walk in his dirty tennis shoes, talking and laughing with the other Africans. He seemed to speak their language perfectly. He'd probably been raised as one of them, Meyerson reflected. It was bad being neither one thing nor the other, despised by every colour in the country, worse even than being a Peruvian.

Then one day the albino walked into the shop and applied for a job. Meyerson was too flustered for a moment to know what to say. As if he thought it might help his request by showing what good manners he had, the albino reached up and took off his old grey felt hat and held it clasped in both hands in front of him. His hair was milky white through which the scalp showed pinkly. The overhead neon lighting danced in his dark glasses with their bright green frames and he shuffled a foot as he waited for Meyerson's response.

He was genuinely taken aback, he had never thought of anybody else doing this work: he ran a shop and what the shop took to run he did. That's all there was to it. He'd never considered anybody else doing the work for him.

'I can sort the stock,' the albino said, 'or I can keep the place clean and neat. I'll do anything. It's not easy for people like me. We're monsters from the bush.' The dark glasses with their hideous green frames flashed at him. 'Give me a break, Mr Meyerson.'

'What's your name?' the chemist asked, to buy time.

'Gus.'

'Well, Gus, I'm sorry, but I don't have no work. This is a one-man show.'

'I could be a delivery boy.'

'I don't deliver,' said the chemist.

'You could if you had me.'

A customer came into the shop. It was Avril Boersma. She had a bad heart and had come in to collect her prescription he'd filled that morning. Her large white legs in their tiny black pumps stomped across the floor. She stared the albino up and down with an inscrutable expression. Meyerson felt deeply embarrassed. Avril Boersma was an important woman: her late husband had been a colonel in the army, and she was prominent in the local school board of governors besides being a woman who attended all his demonstrations of his new lines and bought copiously the products on offer. She leaned her marbled, fleshy forearms on the glass counter and breathed heavily, keeping her eyes on the albino.

'I don't need anybody,' Meyerson snapped. 'Nobody. Now scat.'

'It don't pay to be out in the wild on your own. Think about it.' The albino replaced his hat, pulling it over his ears carefully, and then he turned and walked with great dignity and without looking back, out of the door.

Meyerson shrugged his shoulders. 'An albino.'

'I seen him around, the white nightmare. That's what you get from marriage across the colour lines, Mr Meyerson, mark my words.'

'I reckon it goes hard for people like him. Strangers everywhere.'

Mrs Boersma snorted. 'We don't need things like that here. This is a respectable neighbourhood. What's he want, Mr Meyerson – begging, was it?'

'He wanted to help in the shop.'

Incredulity rippled across her forehead. 'Help you may need, Mr Meyerson, but that walking warning for his father's sins you can do without.'

The subject of assistance came up again when Michaelis gave him advance notice of a new product soon due on the market. 'A sort of home-tanning kit. It's catching on really big in Europe now, they say, and you really can't tell it from the real thing providing you apply it properly.

Smart packaging with choice of roll-on or spray. Secret formula contains a super bronzing agent. It's perfect for your offer of the week. Order in advance and I can get you a good discount, it'd make a beautiful in-store demo, not so?'

Meyerson said he thought it would, only the special offers cost a lot of effort.

Michaelis patted his friend on the shoulder. 'Sure. You're doing the counter at your place – right? And the books, taking the stock, running the prescriptions, and I'll bet doing the deliveries too.'

'We don't do deliveries,' Meyerson said.

Michaelis spooned horseradish onto his roast beef. 'OK, so you're sweeping out, I'll bet. Wise up, Maxie, get in some help.'

The chemist replied that while he could manage himself he preferred it. 'If I took someone on I'd feel I owed him. I don't want to feel beholden to anyone.'

'So don't behold – *employ*,' the fashion buyer retorted. Without asking his friend he sent along the girl. Her name was Maureen Gwass. She'd come to him wanting to be a fashion model but she was dumpy, her ankles were too thick, and so he was passing her on to his old friend who had a good thing going in the cosmetic and styling lines and maybe could use her.

Meyerson stared. When she turned he saw her ankles were rather thick, the calves golden in her best sheer stockings. Then she was dumpy, true, but shapely. And she smiled at him, sweet and full. Her complexion was bright and clear and the auburn hair lay thickly on her shoulders and she thanked him so profusely for giving her 'a leg up in life' that he hadn't the heart to tell her that he didn't need any help.

She began work the next day and he soon felt that she

had changed his life: she wore a white coat and quite of her own accord turned up one morning with large letters embroidered in blue across the shoulders: 'Meyerson's Pharmacy.' She made him tea, she swept out the shop, she tidied the stock-room, she watched with fascinated awe when he dispensed medicines. 'You are a brainy man, Mr Meyerson. I wish I had half of your brain.' Meyerson, delighted with the attention he was getting for the first time in his life, repaid her by giving her little gifts, the small sample bottles of perfume which the travelling salesmen left, trial lipsticks and sachets of shampoo. It was the demonstrations, however, into which Maureen entered with real flair and conviction. There was no longer any need to hire models; it was Maureen's hair that was permed with the week's cut-price offer, Maureen's lips that were painted, Maureen's nails that were varnished. The girl basked under this preening and her delight infused Meyerson with a great sense of pleasure and accomplishment. Soon, he realized, he was desperately in love with her. As for Maureen, her happiness increased by the day. Principally, he saw, because she imagined her small modelling successes were leading her slowly but surely to the stage or the cinema or the television screen, or to whatever glittering venue she had dreamt would one day be her natural place. Meyerson saw the folly of this but said nothing, merely being happy that she was happy.

One evening when Maureen had left and he'd shut up shop for the night and gone upstairs to his room he found the albino stretched in one of his chairs, regarding him blankly from beneath the brim of his felt hat.

'You told me you didn't need an assistant. You told me you weren't giving anybody a job,' the albino said accusingly.

'How did you get in here?'

'You of all people should see that you could have done me a good turn. You're a Jew. You must know what it's like to be out there on your own. Like me.'

'How did you get in here?' Meyerson repeated stupidly.

'Came up the stairs while you were down in the shop. It was easy. If you'd employed me as a security guard, then this wouldn't have happened.'

'Get out or I'll call the police,' said Meyerson.

Gus walked over to the door. 'I'm going. I wouldn't stay where I wasn't wanted.' He made a last attempt. 'You could help me. People like us should stick together. You've got kind eyes. Don't act like a boss.'

'If you're going, go. What are you waiting for?'

'You've locked up downstairs, haven't you? You'll have to let me out. Now, if I worked here I could do that for you.'

Meyerson led the way downstairs and opened the door of the shop and pointed into the darkness.

The albino strode past him. 'That's right. Harden your heart. Throw me out into the night.' The black glasses in their green circles flashed angrily at him.

The albino continued to hang about with the natives who clustered on the pavement in front of the shop, occasionally joining in a game of soccer using an old, bald tennis ball. Meyerson ignored him – so long as he didn't come inside, he told himself, he didn't care what the albino did. But then one day he was in the dispensary checking his drugs cupboard when he heard Maureen scream. Hurrying into the shop he saw her up the ladder, restocking the gift-wrapped bath salts that were specially packed in cut-glass bowls and which he kept for safety on a high shelf. Gus was at the window, his nose pressed up against it, his breath misting the glass through which

Meyerson could see the green circles of his lenses. The albino's nose was white, so hard was it pushed up against the glass, and he was staring straight at Maureen's legs. He hurried Maureen into the back of the shop and calmed her down. When he came out Gus was gone. The chemist's heart seethed with anger against the albino.

'It's just that I've never seen one of them, not a real one, Mr Meyerson. I know they've got pink eyes and funny hair, but I didn't even know what this was, staring at me through the window. There was this face with those funny green rings round its eyes and the nose all squashed up against the window. I feel a real fool now that I know what it is. Shame, poor thing. Imagine what it must be like to be an albino. I mean it's bad enough to be black, but to be – nothing!'

'Don't you waste your sympathy on him. He's got enough cheek to take care of himself.'

'Yes, I know. But just imagine,' Maureen persisted.

He thought no more about the albino until his friend Michaelis delivered the special new line in bronzing agents. He was telling her how the roll-on applicator worked, or if you preferred, how the spray ran a yellow-brown stripe down your forearm. 'It's all the rage, I believe. Except this way you get your tan in the comfort of your own home. You don't have to go to Durban. That's the beauty of it.' Maureen took the can and idly sprayed the back of her hand with it.

'I was hoping you'd see it that way,' Meyerson said, gazing fondly at her plump forearms. 'You'll do it for me, won't you?'

'I wasn't thinking of that. What this needs to show it off at its best is somebody really – white. I was thinking of the albino.'

Instinctively Meyerson recoiled from the idea. It would

mean going back to Gus. It would mean asking him into the shop. It would mean, in effect, giving him a job, going back on everything he had said.

'It's putting him to some good use, Mr Meyerson.'

He looked into the girl's shining eyes and gave way. Not only did he give way, but he astonished himself by going on to praise her brilliant thinking. It was a wonderful idea, it would pull the people in, it would be something they'd never seen before, he really had to hand it to her; in fact, he said, with downcast eyes and a shy smile, he really had been neglecting her, she was far too good and too clever to spend her time replacing stock. Why, he really should make her – his partner. Through lowered lashes he watched to see what effect this had on her and felt her astonished blush to be a great victory.

'Yes,' he said kindly. 'It's putting him to some use.'

The albino's reaction to the offer was not particularly gracious. He haggled over a fee and annoyed Meyerson by insisting on being paid according to the value of what he called his 'time', when it was perfectly apparent that he had more time on his hands than he knew what to do with. And then he insisted on being taken to the shop and shown the products before giving his final consent. Maureen arranged a table in the front window with a white cloth over it on which the range of bronzing agents stood. Gus faced them across the table with his arms folded protectively across his chest, his hat pulled down low over his ridiculous sunglasses. Meyerson demonstrated on Maureen, who was smiling reassuringly at the albino, what he wanted done. The roll-on was to be used on the right forearm and the spray on the left. He didn't intend to cover more than a few square inches, and in this way he calculated that there would be enough skin area on Gus's arm, above and below, to last him for at least three demonstrations.

'Nowhere else,' said the albino slowly, 'I won't be tanned nowhere else. Except only on my hands and arms. Right?'

'Don't you worry about a thing,' Maureen assured him. 'You're in good hands here. We'll look after you.'

'Thanks, Missus. As the only real white man, I need it,' the albino said gratefully.

On the morning of the demonstration Gus arrived promptly and stood before the table rather nervously. Maureen persuaded him to take off his hat. He did so very reluctantly, explaining that to him the sunshine was extremely dangerous. He was one of those who could suffer positive harm by getting a tan. And that meant protecting the top of his head. His scalp, he told her, was tremendously sensitive to sunlight. Maureen sympathized. He had lovely hair, it was like milk.

'It's very thin hair,' said the albino.

'But beautiful. You really ought to show it off.' She took off his jacket and hung it up and then helped him to roll up his sleeves. Around mid-morning with the shop half full of curious onlookers the demonstration of how to give yourself a tan in your own home got under way.

As Maureen had predicted, it was a great success. People came to see the albino as much as to see the product. As Maureen explained to him, Gus was something new and every product needed a gimmick and he was a very rare gimmick, there was nothing really like him, she said. She compared him, after a lot of thought, to a kind of unicorn. Meyerson was thrilled at the success of the scheme, even if he felt that Maureen might have been a little less considerate in her dealings with the albino. She said they had to make allowances. He warned her to be careful, that Gus would only misinterpret her kindness for weakness and exploit her sympathy and her kind woman's heart. He complained about Gus's sunglasses, pointing out to her that it made several small children in the front row very frightened to see the strange man staring blankly back at them and the cheap green frames didn't help either. He counted it as a small success when Maureen agreed with him.

The next day when the albino turned up for the demonstration, Meyerson saw that he was wearing a new pair of sunglasses – a very elegant pair with thin gold frames – and he appeared to have swopped his old felt hat, for he wore in its place a crisp white panama with a red ribbon. On that second morning it was difficult to move in the shop, and when Maureen had rolled the golden colouring onto the albino's right arm and sprayed his left there was ragged applause from the audience, and afterwards Meyerson sold out nearly all his stock.

On the third and last morning the albino arrived attended by a band of Africans who stayed outside and peered through the window. Twice Meyerson chased them away; they only regrouped and returned the moment he re-entered the shop, which was full by mid-morning, and among the audience he noticed Mrs Boersma. Gus entered nonchalantly, tossed his panama onto the counter and allowed Maureen to take his jacket; it was still, Meyerson noticed with satisfaction, the ugly sports coat he'd first seen him in. Then Gus slumped in the chair and held out an arm in a very languid fashion and in the way Meyerson had seen rich women doing in photographs when they went to their manicurists. His anger against the albino mounted. They were all the same. Give them an inch. Meyerson took up a position near the front door where he could both see the proceedings and keep an eye on the excited band of Africans peering through the window. The albino was being quite insufferable. He was quite literally basking in the attention he was being given and in Maureen's solicitous arrangements for his comfort. Meyerson supposed that he couldn't ever in his life have enjoyed this lavish attention. He had a scowling, urgent look about him, an intensity that you caught some sign of in the leaping muscle in his jaw and neck when he rubbed his chin reflectively. Then there was the extraordinary milk-white hair. He'd had a go at persuading Maureen to remove his dark glasses altogether. But she went into the sensitivity of his eyes and the dangers of sunlight and even harsh artificial light and pleaded against it.

'You know, Mr Meyerson, they're really quite pink. Can you believe it?'

Meyerson was aghast at this news. It wasn't the pinkness, he didn't care what colour the albino's eyes were. But he hated the idea that Maureen had seen them.

They ran into their first snag at the demonstration when Maureen discovered there wasn't much flesh left on the arms for her to roll or spray, and even though Gus, with a great show of patience, allowed Maureen to roll his shirt sleeves up to the top of his arms, the audience weren't particularly satisfied. Mrs Boersma spoke for them.

'That's a tanning applicator you've got there, isn't it? Why don't you paint it on his body? Hands and arms are all very well but we get tanned on those when we do our gardening.'

Meyerson acted quickly, striding across the room. 'Will you take off your shirt?' he whispered in the albino's ear.

'I won't. It's not part of the deal, Meyerson. You paid for my arms. My arms you get.'

'It won't hurt, I promise. I'll do it very carefully.' Maureen reached over and squeezed the albino's hand comfortingly.

'I'm up against it,' Meyerson hissed. 'Can't you see they

expect something? If you disappoint my audience, you sabotage my sales. Now take off that damn shirt and let Maureen here put the spray on you. Or you get out of here right now and forget about any money.'

'Certainly not.'

'I'll only do a very little bit,' Maureen told the albino: 'around the shoulders should be enough, the top of the arms, it needn't be more than that. Please. For me.'

The albino reached up and undid the first button.

'For God's sake, get a move on,' Meyerson whispered.

'You think you can do what you like, Meyerson. You think because you're the boss you've got me just where you want me. You think you own this part of Africa so you can do anything.'

Meyerson nodded. 'Yes.' And he felt a bruising, surging joy of that affirmation. 'Yes, I can.'

Gently Maureen drew off the albino's shirt.

The audience clapped and cheered at the icy white, faintly speckled and distantly pink body now emerging into the fluorescent light. Meyerson noticed that Maureen's lips were trembling.

'Give him a spray,' Meyerson ordered.

Maureen raised the can and sprayed a little of the tanning lotion between Gus's shoulder blades.

He writhed. 'It's damn cold!'

'Stand still, dammit!' Meyerson snapped. 'Give him some more.'

Maureen sprayed a straight line down his spine. Her hand was shaking. Gus bellowed again.

'Ladies and gentlemen, see what a lovely gold effect you get,' the chemist rejoiced.

'Turn him round now,' somebody yelled.

'Yes, do him in the front!' Mrs Boersma shrilled.

But the albino had had enough. He was reaching for his

shirt. Maureen stood in front of him, not knowing what to say. The calls for more grew louder. Some in the audience began to stamp their feet. They thought they were being cheated. An atmosphere of mockery was growing and with it grew Meyerson's fury. The albino presented his naked back to the audience; they saw it crossed with golden weals of the spray and he was beginning to pull his shirt back down over his head. Meyerson snatched it away from him and taking the man in a fierce, burly hug he lifted him off his feet, turned him with his chest to the audience and mouthed frantically at the bewildered and astonished Maureen.

'Do him in front.' He could see the agony in her eyes and he repeated his order. The girl stared at him and at Gus, who was struggling frantically, emitting high-pitched little squeals as he tried desperately to break free from the chemist's hug.

'Why doesn't he take off his glasses? We want to see his eyes!' The suggestion was strongly put by somebody in the audience.

Gus's struggles increased in violence.

'For God's sake hurry up, woman,' Meyerson implored.

Duty overcame her softer feelings and Maureen lifted the can, steadying it with both hands in the manner of someone taking very careful aim at a target with a revolver. But in spite of her careful alignment of the nozzle the jet she emitted never reached its target. Or perhaps its target, by now grown wild and frantic, managed somehow to shift his captor, for the spray hit the chemist in the eyes and the blinding pain drove him off the albino and down onto the floor.

It was at this point, he heard later, that the crowd turned really ugly and Gus fled for the door which had been opened by his entranced and amazed black friends who had watched the entire proceedings through plate glass, and Gus, naked to the waist, bare-headed, ran down the street in the sunshine which was so bad for his skin, and that Maureen Gwass, his Maureen, ran after him until at the end of the street, it was said, she stopped and she took off her white chemist's coat, covered his head and shoulders with it and after that they disappeared.

All this they told him, because of course he saw nothing; it was some hours before his eyes, properly treated, dressed and rested, allowed him to see anything at all, and even then for days afterwards, because of some agent in the spray, they were apt, disconcertingly and without warning, to weep great tears.

The incident made Meyerson's name, there was no doubt of that; if before he'd been on the up and up, now he'd achieved the status of a celebrity. Everyone knew him. His turnover doubled. Of Maureen and Gus nothing was heard. They seemed to have disappeared off the face of the earth.

It was his friend Michaelis who one day brought news unexpectedly, when they were dining at the Railway Hotel. He'd actually seen them in a casino, in a neighbouring African state where he had been spending the weekend. He knew Maureen, of course, and he said he recognized her as soon as he saw her, sitting behind the reception desk, where the hostesses who danced with the farmers waited for the customers. She wore an electric-blue dress, he said, with a great white rose at her breast. And Gus, well, he'd seen him when he went to play the tables. Gus was a croupier, his hair now puffed, pomaded, the pale, gleaming pride of the man showed clearly, a bouffant hair-do, Michaelis called it, and of course the fancy dark glasses; he was the preening white peacock of the gaming tables.

'A gimmick, you see. An albino croupier.' There was no

missing the note of grudging admiration. 'I know a gimmick when I see one.'

'Maureen too,' said Meyerson. And he thought to himself, but what life can they have? He saw Maureen, probably blowsy now, in her evening dress and her white rose, and Gus, glossily conceited at his success, the terrible pink skin and the dark glasses, raking chips across the tables. He spoke aloud: 'A gimmick, O.K., but this is something more. I mean it's going native, isn't it?'

Michaelis looked surprised. 'Well, I don't think you could call it that, see what I mean? It's not here, you see, its *there* that they've set up. Still basically bush country, really. Where they are you can do what you like. I mean, it's anyone's country there. Nobody gives a damn. You get my drift? You can do what you like with whoever you like. They think they're getting civilized, what with their independence and their casino. But it's frontier. Raw, bloody frontier.'

Meyerson presided in his shop in the suburb which had a quiet, settled, established look to it. It was almost what you might have called trim. Houses there were sought after because it was convenient for the city centre. He became famous in the suburbs after the albino business. He prospered. And every penny he made was a knife in his heart.

Maggie Running

In the laundromat off Sheridan Square I knew her instantly despite the passage of some twenty years and the fact that she had all her clothes on. I felt again the sun on my skin, squinted in the jagged glare on the quartz-flecked soil where the new, raw houses rose from the dust of the ex-servicemen's estate, where life ended as soon as you were old enough to know it was beginning. All came so sharply back, memories of Africa woundingly incongruous in the wet heat of a New York washhouse. I knew her even in her coat. The little girl beside her looked at me with her mother's eyes. Green eyes? I had always remembered them as blue. So many paintings, so many blue-eyed girls, often naked, always running. Her coat was long, green, unsuitable and buttoned, tightly buttoned from neck to knee.

'Maggie!'

She looked helplessly at her washing breaking through the swirling suds in the machine, pressing against the porthole, streaming back into the foam. There was no escape. The cycle was far from over. Her fingers touched the large buttons. A habit both had, I noticed, touching the carvings as if they were comforted by the feel. Her look appealed to me. I knew how she felt. A strange man with a rough beard, in old blue dungarees and white cotton jacket more suited to a waiter, shouts at you in a washhouse. Waves his hands until he realizes he holds a pair of cooling underpants and stuffs them into his pocket. I understood how she felt but I insisted. The child shrank.

'South Africa!' Removing the offending underwear from my pocket. 'South Africa . . .' pushing it into the drier, 'South Africa – ' The hypnotic steam train rhythm communicated and reassured. She nodded half-understandingly and patted the head of the child.

'Montgomery Street, number twenty-four. The ex-servicemen's estate, I lived next door, remember? My friend lived across the road from you, Tony . . .'

Her eyes widened and then filmed with the effect of concentrating memory, narrowing the mind's eye to focus down the years like a burning glass, hot and white. Something tell-tale smouldered behind her eyes, which took in but did not see the plate-glass shop front where the weak sun slanted across the broken floor tiles, circled the room with its plastic-bag dispensers and advertising banners and the week's cheap soap offers. Something smouldered, but did not take.

'Tony with the yellow hair. He had a sister.'

'Sally?'

'Yes, exactly, Sally . . .' The little girl was blonde and tiny, contemplating me in the shadow of her mother. 'And you have a daughter now.'

'This is my daughter, Estelle.' Her eyes searched my face. The formal acknowledgment increased the distance between us. She could not place me. I don't think she ever did. But she knew where I came from and why. And she remembered Tony. At least I had made the connection. Their coats were identical. Made of some smooth green material, flat as baize and buttoned. Buttons the size of silver dollars, bone incised with geometric patterns and pressed hard and flat against the green which grew around them like grass forced between flagstones. Absurd and unsuitable coats which stopped the eye like a wall. It was ridiculous.

'So now you have a daughter.' Frustration made me say it. I insisted that something had come out of that coat.

'And you are old enough to be your father.'

We were in Tony's garden playing cricket. I was running up to bowl. Sally was fielding and stood by the house, bored and hot, pulling blades of grass. I let go the ball, Tony stepped away from his wicket, Sally spat the chewed blade of grass from her mouth. Tony made no stroke and the ball hit his middle stump. He so clearly didn't care that I was robbed of the pleasure of it. He walked over to the fence and stared across the street with a white face. I joined him at the fence and we both watched Maggie extraordinarily gleaming as she appeared round the corner of the house moving swiftly along the front of the yellow-speckled face-brick with her long brown hair flying behind her. She was thin, and I remember thinking, who knew nothing about these things, that I was reminded of a chicken, a plucked chicken, running. But she was, wasn't she, stark naked in the middle of the afternoon? She must have been mad. Or was I mad? She reached the far corner of the house, rounded it and disappeared. We looked as Sally as one looks pleadingly at some stranger to witness a miracle; she rolled her eyes unhelpfully. She'd seen it too. Tony hissed excitedly. The girl came again, round the corner, moving steadily past the red polished verandah and the front door with the three green panels and the milky glass above, sunlight and shadows sliding across her belly, her clearly visible shoulder blades and then the firm, tiny buttocks; the sunshine when it caught her made the flesh blaze, made us blink and shake our heads though we did not look away. Three times. Or was it four? However many, we knew we'd seen her circle the house, hair streaming, elbows pumping, throwing up her feet, soles gleaming muddily.

After that Maggie was very famous on our estate. It was hard to believe she'd barely been noticed before, a small skinny girl of parents cramped and surly judging by the looks they threw at the neighbours. Generally regarded as not very nice. Maggie stayed indoors most of the time. But when she ventured out what a day it was! She was glorious, she was somebody.

Those brilliant, startling, naked dashes were the making of us, they awoke in us the first glimmerings of the meaning of freedom. Why no one stopped her was a mystery and further testimony to her power, besides being, to our parents, further proof that Maggie's lot were beyond the pale. Her mother I cannot remember. I saw her father, now and then, wrestling a garden from the desert, staking out his beds and planting out his red-hot pokers, a square powerful man with a pink, solidly fleshed face, heavily on his knees in stony soil, building up his rockery against the red dusty street beyond, relentlessly hosing the sparse, fragile patches of green lawn and the uncertain, sickly blooms. Maggie's naked runs threatened life on the estate, drawing black and telepathic judgment from the women, unspoken but final, cruel, unrepeatable. As a result, Maggie's flashing unpredictable nakedness became a children's charm. The potency of this charm lay in the fact that it clearly frightened adults. To say 'I saw Maggie running' earned a hiss, or a slap. Magnificent, fearsome, Maggie scythed through the veils of respectability the new estate attempted to draw around its raw nakedness; fathers pretended not to know, and new young mothers blushed behind their prams; matrons came together and whispered curses.

Carved out of the veld when the soldiers began returning from the desert war up north, the estate was a cheap housing scheme needed to help them settle. Bulldozers, steam rollers and builders moved into the demarcated stretches of country on the edges of the city, and the houses went up, each on its quarter-acre with a lawn space out front and the servants' quarters in the backyard beyond the wash-line by the dust-bins and a garage at the end of the drive, though few had cars. The sandy red streets were given men's names – Michael Street and Sebastian Avenue – and their choking dust blew into the front rooms until you got up some sort of barrier against it, a wall, a split-pole fence, a rockery. Once a week a great water truck sprayed the streets to keep the dust down. The estate lay on a slope running down to a small stream lined with weeping willows; behind the stream a plantation thick with bluegums, and beyond the trees stretched the wild, rocky veld, always obscurely referred to as 'the golf course', though no one played there.

The soldiers coming back from the desert war against Rommel looked at this raw suburb, habit reasserted itself and they began digging in for the duration of their married lives. They'd gone off to fight as boys and came back as family men, and now they battled the ill-made houses and gardens into shape, into what they regarded as proper domesticity, with grim determination and crackling, irritable energy which got the lawns going and kept their wives always pregnant. The eyes of the men were sad and angry and the heavy women puffed as they pushed the prams along the sandy streets. The war had disturbed them profoundly; men who'd never seen the sea went off and fought in foreign parts, girls who'd never said yes for the first time in their lives found it impossible to say no. Then, after the war, sleek-haired fellows with Clark Gable moustaches were met off the troop trains by girls with very red lips and permed hair and pleated skirts and little jaunty hats, and nothing was ever the same again. He went into the insurance office and she put on the bulky disguises of pregnancy. We realized young that this was not what had been anticipated. Yet the fighting spirit lingered, now turned to the effort of establishing themselves, of civilizing the unruly estate as solidly, as finally, as swiftly as possible; the war fever of domesticity gripped the fighters for a place in the sun and a new front lawn of kikuyu grass. Home was to be secured and the ever- present black burglars who infested the estate were to be repelled at all costs. To this end huge and fearsome dogs were bought which were soon attacking dustmen and elderly ladies and children without check. Regrettable but unavoidable casualties of war. Army-issue service revolvers, clean and loaded, waited in the sock drawers of many wardrobes. Some slept with them under their pillows, ready to leap up and blaze away if burglars should come. Many nights I remember my sleep was disturbed by furious gunfire.

The burglars, it was said, came from 'the golf course', slipping through the bluegums at night to attack the sleeping houses with a cunning fishing line and a grasping hook, or duplicate keys obtained from dishonest servants; and the loot, legend held, was carried away in orange sacks.

By day the willows around the little stream and the patchy shade of the bluegums were our playing fields, though we never went into the golf course, where rumour had it that violent men lay in wait, sleeping off their nocturnal raids, liable to attack small boys and knife them. We played at damming the small stream, searched the bluegums for the right forked branches for making catapults and dug clay from the river banks, fixed it in tightly packed balls to the tips of long, flexible willow switches and fought each other, a good flick sending smooth wet gobs flying at the enemy. Sometimes we would come across lead slugs buried deep in the trunks of trees, evidence of bedroom fusillades at midnight.

Battle-weary fathers looked at their children as if they simply couldn't remember where they came from, and perhaps they couldn't, which is not surprising considering the far-off hectic furloughs and passionate leave-takings during which we had been conceived; and our mothers looked only to the babies newly arrived, or on the way, and we, the first-born, felt rather like the children of immigrants who understood nothing of the places their fathers had left behind and didn't particularly care. We soon realized that our new world was small and hot, cramped and dry. We reacted early by becoming wild and a little wicked. We ran behind the big-bellied water trucks that stumbled dribbling and spouting their slow way through the baking streets, a gang of us splashing behind, crazily exultant, rejoicing to see the bone-dry unforgiving dust melting and giving way beneath the spattering impact of these mobile showers flung from the beautifully oozing trucks until great pools lay everywhere filmed with red dust, making, as the feet found, the most lusciously silken mud sliding through clenched toes. After the catapults, the kites, the marbles and the cricket on the front lawns, those water trucks were a great favourite, but the pools they magicked into being on hot afternoons ended all too quickly, dried in the blazing sun and became from one moment to the next sticky, brown, familiar hollows, dried and crusted with mud that you had to skirt your way around and from which you preferred to turn your eyes with something like embarrassment when the sun had done its work. We suffered a nervous dislike for a country that could produce something so soft and silken and forgiving, and reduce it immediately to a cracked, sticky desert before your eyes. Then, like irritable terriers, we hounded the Indian fruit and vegetable man bumping down Henry Street in his green truck, great swatches of brown-paper packets strung from the struts of his open-sided vehicle fanning open in the breeze to reveal, dangling from every hook and eye, fat bunches of onions, bananas and grapes and we followed chanting derisively 'Sammy, Sammy what you got? Missis, Missis apricot . . .'

There was a limit, a clear, narrow limit, to everything. Adults determined to inhabit with a good citizen's proper substance what they sometimes called 'the real world'; ourselves implacably dedicated to destroying it; and so we became more wicked still, stole money from our mothers' purses and spent it on nigger-balls at the corner shop; a boy called Raymond stole his father's service revolver and accidentally shot himself; Derek, my second best friend after Tony, borrowed my bike, which was fourth-hand and had no brakes, and deliberately rode into the concrete fence, flying over the handlebars and smashing head first into the jagged edge, cutting open his forehead, a cut so deep that it showed what looked like a glimpse of bone, and how we stared and whistled as the blood ran down into his eyebrows and dribbled down his chin, dripping into the dust. There was a fierce joy in this I remember, it sweetened the terrible boredom; we stared at the blood-trail he left and heard the screams his mother gave when he reported to the back door, feeling, hoping, that it meant the start of something, that blood, strangely proud of him for having done something apparently worthwhile. It might have been a sign. We were, all of us, waiting for a sign in that province of urchins and burglars, harassed housewives and brooding clerks. We did not know what the sign would be, but we knew it would signify that change was at hand. The appearance of normality was our target; the sense our parents clung to that this was how things ought to be aroused our fury; ingenious, ignorant, dangerous schemes proliferated in our black moments. Derek developed a passion for building houses using the razor-sharp rose and speckled-yellow bricks which littered the estate; every structure he made was taller, broader and more ambitious than the last villa, and all invariably collapsed on the leg or arm or collarbone of some unfortunate guest whom he had invited for a cup of tea from a thermos, or a sausage badly smoked on the outside and still raw after perfunctory immersion in the tiny flames of a green-stick fire; and then Raymond, who came so close to suffocation when the tunnels he dug into the sides of the clay bank with the determination of a mad sapper invariably collapsed when he was well inside, and we'd see his feet sticking out of the mud like lopped branches and would have to pull him to safety in the nick of time; and Tony, who dived into his newly completed swimming pool as it was being filled for the first time, declaring that eight inches of water was more than enough as long as you knew the old circus diver's trick he'd read about in a comic, which was to straighten as you hit the water, only he forgot, or didn't straighten, or the old circus diver had been lying, because he spent the afternoon in bed with a great lump on his head and mild concussion; I for my part became a pyromaniac and took to lighting fires everywhere; I went round with my pockets stuffed with boxes of matches, rattling like a Mexican dance band and setting angry, spitting blazes in the garage, in the woods, behind the servant's room. It never amounted to anything, of course, all our wickedness, our self-destructiveness. It petered out, rather in the way my fires did, leaving a few scorch marks, a few bruises, perhaps a headache, a scar, a little ash. Everything stifled under the ferocious regime of orderliness and ennui; we went forward eagerly and openly to attack it and found ourselves censured, depressed under the familiar thumb of meagre circumstance. At times like these it seemed we were lost forever, the sky lowered and leaned upon us and shrank our little world into a few dirt streets on which the mud dried faster as we grew older, after a magic passing of the water trucks with their water wands had set the world briefly free and running.

It was then, with that extraordinary instinct for timing, that Maggie emerged to save us, running round the corner of the house, naked as the day she was born, astounding the world and setting it flowing.

I don't think I ever spoke to her, but her daring and the intense disapproval it evoked in the minds of our parents made her quite wonderful to us. Did she leave the estate first? Perhaps we went first. We all went sooner or later; as soon as our fathers 'got things under control' they declared the war won and moved out. The battle turned out to be everything. The peace was not for them. I've never again met anyone from the estate – not, that is, until I saw Maggie in the laundromat.

I have my subject; I may paint water, or ships, or children, but they are alike. Sketches, montage, full portraits, brief studies celebrate my theme. Running women appear unexpectedly in the corners of canvases which seem to have very different aims. Flowing water is everywhere in my work. These are my gestures of appreciation, for my art if it is anything is a form of gratitude. Running women, running water – they release and free my imagination. Meeting the well-wrapped, bulky, nervous woman in the laundromat who freed me I wished to thank her personally. I insisted on it.

As we walked down Christopher Street with the little girl tagging on behind, all of us carrying our bulging bags of laundry, we were silent. Around here, too, too many streets have men's names. The glittering shopfronts crammed with treasures, tit-bits, tasty morsels cast on the water for the shoals of hungry tourists swimming past: tiny exquisite Dutch dolls with varnished foreheads and scarlet lips; a fragile confusion of ingenious and delicate Japanese papercraft lovingly displayed; handmade rocking horses from Vermont with scarlet pommels and nut-brown, varnished hooves; copies of old Ibo masks looking down their long, straight noses; French music hall posters, legs and frothing petticoats. All bait, succulent, spruced and gleaming, irresistibly bright, good enough to eat, painted, coloured, lacquered, cunningly delicious as trout flies to the people mouthing hungrily alongside the plate glass, nosing towards the pretty lures. It was understandable in people who had no Maggie running. They must have something and so took this bait open-mouthed. It was only human. Maggie didn't look in the windows, she bent her head and marched on purposefully, black bag clutched to her side, her shoulders moving in the thick hairy coat. I was forced to break her deliberate silence.

'What are you doing in America?'

She gave a grave, apologetic smile, stopped and, as if to fortify herself, took out a green silk headscarf, tied it firmly around her square face and knotted it cruelly under the chin. She cast several nervous glances at the big blue plastic bag in which I was carrying my laundry. 'I married an American. He came to South Africa, a kind of salesman he was. We met in Port Elizabeth. He was selling his stuff in those new hotels that were going up all around the coast, bar novelties. His name was Rolf. Beer mugs with distant views of Ben Nevis that were really jig-saw puzzles, fake rubber olives that bounced and strange glasses in which you saw naked women when you poured your gin, and any number of swizzle sticks.'

'Shaped like pitch-forks,' Estelle volunteered. The child had crept nearer to us as we walked.

'Tridents. They were tridents.' In the scarf, Maggie's square face was her father's. 'He wasn't a bad father, Rolf. He got on well with the child, well I mean he would, wouldn't he? He liked playing with toys. It's not enough, though. He was a simple man,' she added, dropping her voice and glancing round at the child skipping happily behind us, 'small with very yellow hair and a good deal of energy. But that doesn't help. Not when you've got to feed a family. Full of dreams. He imagined he was in frontier country where a man could do anything. I suppose you could say he came to Africa and went mad. And we owed money. Both happen.'

'You came back here?'

Maggie nodded. 'We had an apartment full of toys. Crazy birds with red felt heads and glass bodies that you stand on bars and watch them endlessly dunking their beaks into glasses of water, and thousands, I don't exaggerate, thousands of plastic coasters with pictures of German castles. He owed money again. One day he was in Vermont investigating a new Japanese line in floating flowers that blossomed in your vermouth, when his creditors got an order against him. They came for the furniture. I phoned him in Vermont. He said not to worry, he knew exactly what to do.' The heavy head, helmeted in silk, swung towards me. 'He fled back to South Africa. Can you believe it? Last I heard he was working for one of those giant hotels they'd put up in the Native reserves and he was a big noise, general manager, pizzas. He says he's made it at last. He even sends me money sometimes.'

On McDougall Street, with its scatter of restaurants where the Old Liberal Club once stood, a water-main had burst. We slowed as we approached the flood.

'What are you doing now?'

'I'm a painter.'

The look Maggie gave me mingled disbelief and sympathy in about equal parts and left me feeling distinctly uneasy.

'What else do you do?'

'I don't do anything else.'

'God, man, that's hard.' The South African accent came out broad and brisk.

For perhaps twenty-five yards the street was submerged, a paltry, shallow-water Venice; reflected in the water the city shivered and quaked, all its sharp planes and angles were liquified, its certainties quivered and could not sustain their sense of importance. We stood at the water's edge and the city trembled beneath us.

I bent down and began to unlace my shoes. The little girl pressed close, her eyes wide. 'It's years since I had a chance to do this.' I rolled my trousers to the knees.

The little girl began to take off her shoes, ignoring her mother's remonstrations.

'You'll get your feet all dirty going through there.'

The child gazed at the backs of my legs. 'You look funny like that.'

'Well, in that case I'm glad you're coming with me. We can look funny together.'

'At least give me your bag, Estelle.' Her mother took the bag from the child. 'I'm going to walk round. I'll see you on the other side.'

I put Estelle's socks and shoes in my pocket, and taking her hand we waded into the water, staring down and watching the small waves breaking at our ankles. The water was clear and our feet very white and the feel of the macadam still warm from the sun, slightly gravelly and not unpleasant. Estelle walked with great concentration as if she were on a tightrope or a narrow bridge and might fall off before she got to the other side. Her lips were pale with excitement.

'I've never done this before.'

'I haven't done it for years and years, not since I was as small as you are, perhaps smaller.'

'Could you do it whenever you wanted?'

'We could do it whenever the water truck came. The streets where I lived were plain sand, red dust, and it was often very hot in the summer, and to keep the dust blowing off the streets and into the houses the trucks used to come once or twice a week and spray the streets. They left enormous pools behind and we always used to get together and run into these pools digging our toes into the mud and splashing each other. It was great fun.'

'You can't take off your shoes here.'

'In Africa lots of people do, you see them going around barefoot all the time.'

She carolled her astonishment. 'All the time! Did my mother do it?'

Once through the water we sat on a kerb and I dried her feet with my jacket and helped her on with her socks and shoes. Around the corner Maggie hove into view, moving steadily, humping the two bags of laundry, deep inside her strange coat, the sun gleaming on her headscarf.

'Ask her yourself,' I said to Estelle.

'Did you go barefoot in Africa – when the water truck came?'

'I hope you dried between your toes before you put your socks on.'

We all picked up our laundry bags and followed Maggie. Again I was forced to speak. 'You used to go running. Running round your house. Do you remember?'

Carefully she lowered the bags to the ground. 'Yes, I

remember. But you don't. You're a man. You never thought.'

'Thought of what?'

'Of my father.'

I thought of her father then, looking at his daughter. I saw him down the long tunnel, tiny, busy, building his rockery.

'I wasn't running.'

'But you did. We saw you.'

She picked up her bags and walked on, smiling for the first time. 'Not running,' she repeated deliberately, 'chased.' She ushered Estelle before her bending her head in its solid scarf over the child in the way her father must have done, lowering his meaty face over the flowers in his hot, hopeless garden. And I saw that as she walked she was moving now inside the coat.

They lived in one of the tall ugly towers which have been striding into the Village for years. I left them at the door of their apartment on the third floor. Maggie was almost relaxed. There was in the swing of the two bags a feeling that they were no weight at all. She gave the impression that she might even have talked to me, after that – if I could have thought of anything to say. Memory was returning like a half-forgotten scent and she was tasting again the old power, the smashing magic which had made adults tremble and spit. She gave me her hand. Firm and strong. A man's grip. The little girl looked at me with her mother's eyes.

At the corner of the street I turned. They were at the window watching me. It was my impression – though of course I dare not insist on it – that they had taken off their coats.